NEW ORLEANS
HOMICIDE

BY

John C Dalglish

2018

NEW ORLEANS HOMICIDE

John C Dalglish

NEW ORLEANS HOMICIDE

Sunday, January 28

Lakeshore Drive
Lake Pontchartrain
North New Orleans
1:45 a.m.

He was in no particular hurry, but he kept pace with the light traffic around him as he traveled east along Lakeshore Drive. The purpose of this trip did not require him to be at his destination by a certain time…only that he finished his task before the morning light.

To his left, Lake Pontchartrain stretched out some six hundred-plus square miles. Every time he passed by the brackish water, his mind would play back a song by the band Poco, as if someone had dropped a coin in his mental jukebox.

> In the heart of the night
> In the cool southern rain
> There's a full moon in sight
> Shinin' down on the Pontchartrain

The lyrics described this night perfectly.

He passed by the Mardi Gras Fountain, now refurbished like so many other things since Hurricane Katrina. A bridge took him over Bayou St. John, and within less than three minutes, he reached the London Avenue Canal. Turning right on Pratt Drive, he pulled alongside London Park and stopped.

The large, grassy area dotted with trees was a popular spot for picnickers and dog walkers during the day. The park's east border pressed up against the London Avenue Canal, with a large berm rising at the edge of the water. He shut down the van and cut his lights.

The light rain and early morning hour practically guaranteed he wouldn't have company, but he was not one to take chances. Sitting in the darkness, his right hand resting on his package, he listened to the light tapping of raindrops on the roof of his vehicle. While he would seem relaxed to a passerby, his eyes scanned the area with intensity and precision. Any movement needed to be examined and identified before he committed to getting out of his van.

After more than twenty minutes, he pulled the door handle, grabbed a duffle bag, and with the interior light of his van disconnected, he slid unseen into the darkness. His senses reaching out around him, he now moved quickly and with purpose. This was no time to be seen, no place to be stopped.

He reached the top of the berm, opened the bag, and removed a two-gallon plastic jug.

Closing his eyes, he muttered to himself, moving his lips but making no sound. When he was done, he uncapped the jug, tipped it gently, and began pouring the contents into a strip along the top of the berm. No more than ten steps later, he'd emptied the jug, and stopped.

After quickly re-capping the jug and tucking it back inside the duffle bag, he headed toward his vehicle. Just seven minutes after getting out, he was back inside the van and driving away. As he turned west on Lakeshore Drive, a smile came to his face.

As if on cue, the Poco song started in his head again. This time, he sang along.

Old Gentilly Road
Venetian Isles
East New Orleans
6:30 a.m.

Clay Morris steered his big rig off I-10 and turned south onto Paris Road. Technically, Paris Road was part of I-510, but he'd grown up calling it Paris, and that was how most locals referred to it. Rubbing his eyes, he attempted to clear the bleariness that had set in during the last ten hours on the road.

NEW ORLEANS HOMICIDE

Driving all night, he'd made it in from Oklahoma City and dropped his load. Now, he was headed to the terminal and then to attend his son's birthday party. The sun was just peeking over the horizon as he reached the exit for Old Gentilly Road. He followed the exit around to Almonaster Avenue, turned right, and reached Old Gentilly.

As he turned east, the rising sun's glare forced him to squint when he entered the Southwest Freight yard. As he straightened out, something glinted from down in the roadside ditch. His rig was moving slowly enough that he got a decent look at it.

Is that a manikin?

A second glance suggested someone sleeping, their hands crossed on their chest.

Who would sleep in a ditch?

He'd seen a lot of weird stuff as an over-the-road driver but this was stranger than usual.

After Pulling into the trucking yard, and despite his exhaustion, his curiosity got the better of him. Dropping slowly from the cab, he stretched his arms toward the sky then arched his back in a futile attempt to release ten hours of stiff muscles. Shuffling his feet in the gravel, he made his way to the ditch where he'd spotted the shape and peered down.

In the growing light, the pale skin and long black hair gave it the appearance of an oversized child's doll. His gaze moved to the manikin's eyes. Open and blank, they stared through a milky haze toward the brightening sky.

The hair on the back of his neck stood up. They were unlike any manikin's eyes he'd ever seen.

Then he caught sight of the wrists—slashed and stained red.

Manikins don't bleed!

In an instant, realization washed over him. He was staring at a dead body. Stumbling backward, he fell, scrambled to his feet, then ran toward the terminal. In his panic, he fell again. Dragging himself back to his feet for the second time, he staggered to the office door and threw it open.

A startled secretary looked up at him. "What the...?"

"Call 9-1-1!"

Her forehead creased as confusion painted itself across her face. "What?"

"Call 9-1-1! There's a dead body by the road!"

Her gaze went to the door then back to him. "A body?"

Frustrated, he grabbed the phone on the desk.

"9-1-1. What is your emergency?"

"A body!"

"A dead body?"

He was too tired for this. "Yes, a dead body!"

"Very well. Where are you?"

"Southwest Freight on Old Gentilly."

Southwest Freight Terminal
Venetian Isles
East New Orleans
8:10 a.m.

Nikki Santiago pulled up at the terminal and put her car in park. Grabbing her long brown hair, she pulled it into a ponytail and double-wrapped an elastic band around it. Glancing in the rearview mirror, her dark-brown eyes were less bloodshot than she'd feared. Lack of sleep usually turned her eyes into red roadmaps. She decided she looked pretty good for someone working on three hours sleep.

Turning to the scene in front of her, she studied it carefully, just as her mentor had taught her.

His words echoed within her. Learn as much as you can before even exiting the vehicle.

A three-year veteran of Major Crimes, she had recently lost her partner to retirement and was still without a replacement. Not that she minded working cases solo, but it did mean she had to do everything. No sharing the burden and dividing the work, and no one to bounce ideas off of.

Of course, she wasn't in an unusual position. Most detectives were working solo because of short staffing across the department, a problem that persisted more than a decade after Katrina.

The responding officers had stretched yellow crime tape, which encompassed a large area of the freight yard. Most of the activity was focused on the drainage ditch that ran across the front of the yard, and both the coroner and the forensic team had arrived before her.

She scanned the road leading to the freight yard. Old Gentilly was primarily a commercial route, with a semi-truck maintenance yard to the west and another freight facility to the east. The road was easily accessible from multiple directions via several major thoroughfares. Before stepping out of the car, she guessed this was a dumpsite.

Stepping out of the car, she re-tucked her long-sleeved navy-blue shirt into her pin-striped black pants. Reaching into the back seat, she extracted her department jacket and pulled it on against the morning chill. Late January mornings were typically in the upper forties or lower fifties, and this day was no exception.

The on-duty sergeant was the first to notice her arrival. He approached her, his expression grave, and she sensed he'd been shaken by what he'd seen.

"Detective Santiago?"

"Yes."

"I'm Sergeant Butler. One of my officers was first on scene."

"What have we got?"

He sighed. "Female, black, twenties, DOA, probably dumped."

"Any identification?"

He shook his head. "Not so far."

"Who found the body?"

Banks turned and pointed at a man leaning next to a big rig.

"His name is Clay Morris. He'd just come in off the road and thought he'd seen a manikin."

"Poor guy. Any witnesses?"

"Not yet."

She stared down the road in both directions. "Let's get officers knocking at businesses, and I want everyone who was at this terminal in the last twenty-four hours interviewed."

"Yes, ma'am."

"Thank you, Sergeant."

As he left, Nikki spotted a familiar face coming toward her. Coroner Chris Nagle gave her a small wave.

"Morning, Nikki."

"Hi, Doc. Working a Sunday?"

He nodded. "I try to every month or so, just on principle."

She liked that. Nagle believed they were all part of a team, with each person as important as the next. At thirty-nine, a relatively young age for the position he held, Chris was widely respected across the state for the way he ran his department.

She smiled. "Well, I, for one, am always glad to see you."

"Thank you kindly."

His receding hairline and bright-blue eyes were usually accompanied by a smile, even at the grimmest of scenes. He had insisted he didn't want the work to define him and once told her that the funniest people he'd ever met were funeral directors.

Though skeptical, she had grinned. "I'll take your word for it."

"No, I'm serious. Behind closed doors, they have a wicked sense of humor."

She remained unconvinced, but Chris was one of the most pleasant people she had ever come across. She glanced toward the body still hidden below the lip of the ditch.

"I got the basics from the sergeant. He suggested she may have been dumped."

"I would agree; in fact, I'd say it's a certainty."

"Oh? Why?"

He started to tell her then stopped. "Follow me."

A chill crept up her spine as she tailed the coroner over to where the victim lay. He was not normally mysterious. A forensic photographer was busy shooting pictures but stopped when Chris climbed down into the ditch.

Her first impression of the body, although fully dressed, was that the victim had died in her sleep. Her clothing was clean—running shorts, a red t-shirt, and sneakers—and her only jewelry was a gold chain around her neck that sparkled in the sunlight.

The idea that the girl was asleep quickly disappeared when Nikki saw how pale her face was. She'd seen her share of corpses, most of which had *some* color from the congealing blood, but this one... Her brain seized, unwilling to accept her next thought.

Nagle stared back at her, his finger pointing at the wrists. Her voice failed her.

Evidently, Nagle saw the recognition on her face. He lifted one of the girl's arms for Nikki to get a better look at the wound. The deeply carved X-mark across the radial artery was unmistakable.

He let the arm return to its position.

Nikki finally got her tongue to move. "You think it's him?"

"I do. It all fits."

He was right, of course. There could be no other conclusion.

While the cause of death, blood loss, had been revealed to the press, the place and shape of the cuts had been kept secret. Also, the fact that *all* the blood had been drained from the body had been kept under wraps.

Those facts eliminated a copycat, and the idea that two people coincidentally had the same M.O. was unlikely at best. Then there was the time of the year—the Mardi Gras parades were just getting started.

Her next thought was of her ex-partner, Vince.

NEW ORLEANS HOMICIDE

Office of Lieutenant Terrell Baker
Major Crimes Division
715 South Broad Avenue
Mid-City
8:45 a.m.

Lieutenant Ted Baker hung up his coat behind his desk and twirled his chair to sit down. He was heavier now than when he worked the streets, the muscles in his chest having morphed into fat and settled near his waist. Like his waistline, his moustache was fuller, as well, and tinged with gray. The only thing that had gotten thinner was his hair, and so he'd shaved his head. It was cooler in the stifling humidity of a New Orleans summer, anyway.

The highest-ranked African-American in Major Crimes, he was not prone to worry. That trait had served him well in his twenty-two years at the New Orleans PD. Rising from a beat officer to become head of the homicide division, his motto had never changed: *worry comes from not being prepared.*

He had worked harder than most at examining possibilities, considering outcomes, and predicting the best path in each situation. It was a skill—or as some saw it, a talent—he tried to imprint upon all the men and women serving under him. He'd had varying degrees of success, but Nikki Santiago seemed to grasp the concept better than most.

That was why her phone call, indicating she needed to see him immediately, had come as a surprise.

He pushed his rimless glasses up on his nose just as a light knock came at the door.

"Come!"

John C Dalglish

The brown hair, brown eyes, and round face of Santiago peered through a crack in the door. "I'm not interrupting anything?"

He waved her in. "Nothing. Sit down."

He studied her as she opened the door just wide enough to get through then closed it softly behind her. Nikki was unlike most of the other women on his detail. The abrasive edge and hard-charging attitude, which seemed to be a prerequisite for the job, were not part of her make-up. Instead, she was pensive, measured, and above all, smart.

He waited until she had settled into her seat, then smiled. "Good morning."

"Morning, sir."

"You just came from a scene, correct?"

She nodded. "Over on Old Gentilly near Paris Road."

"Did you run into a problem?"

"No—no problem. At least, not exactly."

He smiled, extending to her a measure of patience he sometimes didn't give other detectives. She was his newest charge, but even so, he respected her need to formulate opinions.

"So what was it you needed to see me about?"

"Well, sir…I wanted you to be aware…that is, I thought you should know immediately…"

This was the most flustered he'd seen her since she was told Vince was retiring.

"Focus, Nikki."

She managed a weak smile. "Yes, sir."

She took a deep breath, and her eyes came up to meet his. "I feel—and Chris Nagle agrees—that the Mardi Gras killer is back."

He stared at her blankly, his heartrate escalating as his mind raced through a series of photos. Each picture of the same crime scene. Eight in all. For the first time in a long time, he found himself unprepared.

"Nagle agrees with you?"

"Yes. The scene is a mirror image of the previous ones, and the timing is right."

"The injuries?"

"Identical."

He leaned back in his chair, stared at the ceiling, and drew in a deep breath.

"Sir?"

He looked at her. She was going where his mind already was.

"I would like to ask if we could…"

He held up a meaty hand, stopping her before she could finish.

"You go back to the scene and continue working it. I'll talk with the chief and let you know what he decides."

She stood. "Very well."

"And Nikki?"

"Sir?"

"Thank you."

She nodded and slipped back out of the office.

He picked up the phone and dialed. As he expected, Stella Jacobs answered, she served as call screener on her husband's days off. Her melodic voice had a sing-song quality.

"Hello?"

"Hi, Stella. It's Ted."

"Good Morning. Glen isn't here at the moment."

"Do you expect him soon?"

"He went after the morning paper at Rouses."

Rouses Grocery wasn't far from the captain's home, but that didn't mean the boss would be returning soon. Captain Jacobs was renowned for his pension to roam the aisles in flea markets and stores alike. At Rouses, Jacobs could spend a long time checking out the hand-rolled sushi, fresh seafood, and anything else that caught his fancy. He might return in ten minutes or two hours.

"Have him call me?"

"Of course."

"Thanks."

Home of Vincent and Rose Wills
Memphis Street
Lakeview Neighborhood
North New Orleans
11:45 a.m.

Vince Wills unlocked the front door, then held it open for his wife. He and Rose had just returned from church, and his wife had not worn a warm enough coat. She stepped past him and went straight toward the kitchen to make coffee.

He closed the door and removed his jacket. Following her into the kitchen, he focused in on finding something in the fridge to eat. Swinging both upper doors of the French door model wide open, he stood staring at the contents.

Like the home itself, the fridge was relatively new. After Katrina, virtually every home in the neighborhood had been rebuilt from the ground up. Their single-story, stick-built structure had been washed away, and though they had considered moving to a different part of the city, ultimately, they had decided this neighborhood was home.

So, though it took several years, their new house had risen on the same lot. This model was concrete and brick, with two stories instead of one. He missed the simplicity of their old place but liked the solid feel of the new one.

"It's not going to crawl out and cook itself, Vince."

He turned to see her watching him with the big brown eyes that had captured him nearly forty years ago. Her hair was shorter now, a pretty mixture of silver and gray, and like him, she had put on a few pounds. She was still the most beautiful woman he's ever seen. Her full lips were curled up in a teasing smile.

He laughed. "One can always hope."

"Hope what? That your wife will come push you out of the way and make something?"

"Maybe."

She crossed the kitchen and kissed him on the cheek, while prying the doors loose from his grip at the same time. "You can wait like everyone else. The kids will be here soon, and we'll eat together."

"But…"

"Don't you 'but' me, Vincent Wills."

Resistance was futile. He kissed her forehead and got himself a cup of coffee instead. Before he could raise the cup to his lips, his cell phone rang. A photo of his old friend and boss, Ted Baker, lit up his screen.

He pushed answer. "Hi, Ted."

"Hey, Vince. How ya doin'?"

"Good."

"How's Rose?"

Vince glanced at his wife, who was carrying her cup of coffee toward the living room.

"Our girls are coming over for the granddaughter's birthday, so she is great."

His friend laughed. "She loves her girls."

The tone of his friend's voice said this was not a social call. Vince's mind went to the many friends he had in the department, suddenly concerned Ted had called with sad news.

"What is it, Ted?"

Another half-hearted chuckle. "You know me too well."

Vince waited.

"I'm sorry to interrupt your day, but there's something I thought you should know."

"Which is?"

"We think he's back."

Vince's face flushed, and his heartrate doubled. There was no need to ask who the *he* was. For a moment, the room spun, and Vince thought he would be sick.

He took in a long, slow breath, forcing himself to focus. "Are you sure?"

"Nikki was the responding detective, and Chris Nagle was there."

They were the two people who were most qualified to identify the M.O.

Vince stole a look into the living room. Rose was reading the paper and fortunately, had not been watching him when he answered the phone.

This call was one both of them had hoped would never come. In fact, he might not have retired if the case wasn't as cold as it had been when he left. Most believed, or hoped, the killer was gone, dead, or incarcerated—anything but still out there.

"Vince?"

"I'm here. Thanks for letting me know."

"There's something else."

"Okay."

"Would you be willing to come back on for the investigation?"

Emotions washed over him, a flood that consisted of both anxiety and relief.

Part of him seemed to dread the idea, but another part was relieved he'd been asked.

One thing was certain, the question didn't surprise him.

He looked again at Rose. There was no doubt which side she would come down on.

"What did Jacobs say?"

"He was reluctant at first—he believes you should respect an officer's retirement—but he agreed with my sentiment."

"Which was?"

"You're our best chance of catching this guy—maybe our only chance."

"Santiago knows the case as well as I do."

"The facts, sure, but she doesn't know the guy. You have the experience of chasing him. You know his psyche. He'll have killed and be back in hiding before anyone else can get up to speed on the case, even with your former partner's help."

That was true. But it was also true that the last six months had been good for him and Rose. She wouldn't be happy about him going back, but more than that, she might be hurt by it. Her well-being was just as important to consider as his desire to catch the killer.

"I don't know, Ted."

"Look, I know this is a big ask on my part. Will you consider it? I wouldn't ask if I didn't think it was a matter of life and death."

Another true statement. At least two more women would die, maybe more.

"I have to discuss it with Rose."

"Of course. Let me know soon?"

"I'll let you know when I do."

There was a brief pause. "Thanks."

"Bye, Ted."

Vince hung up and swallowed hard, preparing himself to face Rose. He changed his mind and picked his phone back up, hitting speed dial.

"Hi, Vince."

"Hi, Nikki."

"I gather you've spoken with the lieutenant?"

"Just got off the phone."

She waited him out, apparently aware of what was coming next. He needed to hear it from her, not his boss. He cleared his throat.

"Is it him?"

"Yes."

"You're sure?"

"As sure as I can be."

"Nagle thinks so, too?"

"Yes."

He sighed. "Okay. Talk later."

He hung up without waiting for a goodbye.

Just as he put his phone down, the front door opened.

NEW ORLEANS HOMICIDE

Major Crimes Division
715 South Broad Avenue
Mid-City
2:15 p.m.

Four hours later, Nikki had finally been able to leave the crime scene and return to her desk. She had work to do, but the biggest thing on her mind was news about her old partner. She had repeated a silent mantra numerous times since her conversation with the lieutenant: *Please let Vince come back.*

It wasn't that she didn't feel she could work the case, nor was she afraid of tracking the killer—that was her job. Her anxiety came from something else—watching Vince work the case for the past three years. In that time, his burden had grown, his steps had got a little slower, and his mind a little less focused.

On the day he retired, Vince Wills was still the best detective she'd ever met—or probably would ever meet—in her law enforcement career, but the unsolved case had taken its toll on her mentor. She wasn't sure if Vince had recognized the weight he carried, but she wasn't surprised when he told her he was considering retirement. She'd been caught off guard, though, by how fast it came about.

So now, she found herself hoping he would come back to work the case, partly for selfish reasons, and partly for Vince. She feared the case might exact a similar toll on her as it had on him, but more than that, she wanted him to have the chance to unload the burden of the biggest unsolved case of his career.

The door to the lieutenant's office had been closed since she got back, but from her desk, she could see it swing wide now. Baker stuck his head out and looked in her direction.

"Santiago?"

"Sir?"

"Moment of your time, please."

She rose immediately and crossed the squad room. Only two other detectives were there on that Sunday afternoon, but she sensed both sets of eyes following her. When she stepped into the office, the lieutenant was already sitting back behind his desk.

"Close the door."

She did then sat.

He laced his fingers together, leaned forward, and met her gaze. "Effective immediately, your sole focus is the Mardi Gras case. Your other cases will be reassigned."

"Yes, sir."

"I've spoken with Vince and asked him to come aboard for the investigation. We all know the clock is ticking, and though the chief wasn't thrilled, he signed off on the request."

Her hopes surged. "I understand. What did Vince say?"

Baker leaned back in his chair, taking his laced fingers and putting them behind his head. His gaze moved to the ceiling, as if looking for a message from above.

"He said he would talk with Rose and get back to me. I wish I could say my gut tells me he will be back, but I'm just not sure, partly because I'm not certain what I would do in his situation."

"I would think the chance to solve the case might be an incentive."

"Indeed, and as a young detective, I saw things the same way…"

She waited for the *but*.

"But as time passes, you learn that the detective badge bears a heavy weight, and once taken off, it can be very tough to put it back on."

Her optimism waned. "He knows this guy better than anyone."

He smiled. "That's exactly what I told him. You should know he thought you could handle the case without him."

The statement didn't surprise her. If she'd heard it once from Vince, she'd heard it a thousand times.

"You're good, Nikki. Don't look to me for the answers. I wish I had been as good as you are when I was your age."

She smiled. "He's just trying to pass the buck."

Baker laughed. "Maybe, but it's true. And for now, you're in charge."

Her heart leaped into her throat. *In charge* meant responsible—not just for leading the case—but for the lives that hung in the balance. She swallowed hard.

"Yes, sir."

He rocked forward, his smile disappearing.

"I want everything we have on our killer brought to the conference room. Go through it, and organize it the best you can. Operate under the assumption that your partner will be back, and set it up as if you were getting it ready for him."

"And if he doesn't?"

"Then you will be assigned all the help you need, and you'll brief them, instead. Understood?"

"Yes, sir."

"Good. Dismissed."

Nikki rose from her seat, hoping her nerves did not betray her. If this case fell on her, then she would do her best. As she left the office, she said her mantra one more time.

Home of Vincent and Rose Wills
Memphis Street
Lakeview Neighborhood
North New Orleans
3:25 p.m.

Vince held the digital camera at the ready, waiting for Rose to carry the cake into the dining room. Their daughters, Alicia and Dominique, were standing next to the table.

Domm's daughter, Grace, sat at the head of the table with a wide smile. Turning six, Grace was the spitting image of her mother at the same age. Sparkling green eyes, curly brown hair—tinged with red—that hung past her shoulders, and a smile that never quit. Her attitude was the same as her mother's, too, which gave Vince pause.

Domm had always been the type to go headlong into everything. She didn't just have a boyfriend, she was in love. She didn't just want the car, she had to have it. She wasn't only unhappy at her job, but it was eating her soul.

His old partner Nikki had once described that attitude fittingly, saying, "Domm likes going ninety miles an hour with her hair on fire."

And that same attitude had led to the birth of Grace. Domm was in love, she and her new guy were going to get married, and they wanted a family. So, as with many young couples, the cart got put before the horse. Grace was born but the relationship died.

That was all water under the bridge now, and Grace was the light of his and Rose's world.

23

"Everyone sing!" Rose appeared at the kitchen door, carrying a round cake bearing six burning candles. "Happy birthday to you…"

Vince left the singing to the women while he snapped multiple shots of the ceremony. As always, his wife was the boss.

"Make a wish, Grace."

The little girl squeezed her eyes real tight then let them spring open again. "Done!"

"Blow out the candles!"

Extinguished candles were followed by applause.

Rose looked over at him. "Did you get it?"

"I believe so."

"Good."

The cake was cut and doled out, and Vince took his into the living room. Lowering himself into his chair, cake in one hand and coffee in the other, he watched as Grace smeared cake on her mother's nose. His heart was full, and more than any time in his life, he recognized how lucky he was.

Of course, that made the decision much harder. He just wasn't sure he could do it.

Alicia came over and sat next to him. "Hey, Daddy."

"Hey, yourself. I haven't had a chance to ask you, but how are your studies going?"

"Good."

Alicia was the opposite of her baby sister. *Serious from the crib* was how Rose described their eldest daughter.

Alicia was studying at Tulane, working on her Master's in Molecular Biology. It seemed obvious to Vince that she got her smarts from her mother since he could barely spell molecular. She had also been graced with her mother's jet-black hair, perfect skin, and innate ability to recognize people's emotions.

Apparently, she was using the latter trait at that moment. "Everything okay with you?"

As a detective, he was an expert at avoiding the point. "With me? Sure, why?"

As usual, it didn't work with Alicia any more than it did with Rose. "Just seems like something is bothering you, that's all."

He smiled. "Don't worry about me. You focus on your studies."

She rolled her eyes. "Yes, sir."

She picked up his plate and added it to hers, kissed him on the forehead, and went toward the kitchen. If Alicia had sensed his mood, there was no doubt his wife would know something was up. He looked at the clock. The girls would be leaving soon, which meant the time was coming to tell Rose.

But tell her what? That he wanted to go back? Or that he wanted to stay with her, and let someone else have their shot?

He finally decided to let Rose have the final say. He trusted her judgment more than anyone else's.

But first, he had to tell her.

****

Rose Wills kissed her granddaughter once more before closing the door. She returned to the kitchen, where she put away the remaining gumbo from dinner. Vince was sitting at the dinner table, the digital camera in front of him.

"You want a glass of wine, Vince?"

"Sounds good."

She retrieved two goblets from the cabinet and poured them each some of their favorite red. Glasses in hand, she joined him at the table.

"Get any good ones?"

He nodded and turned the camera so she could see the screen. "Look at Grace blowing out her candles. Doesn't she look exactly like Domm?"

Rose sipped her wine and examined the photo. It was a well-established fact that Grace looked like her mother, further cementing Rose's belief that her husband was stalling. She set her glass on the table and slowly rolled the stem between her fingers, her gaze fixed on her husband.

She'd struck it rich when she snagged Vincent Stanley Wills. Not because he was handsome, though with his puppy-dog eyes and deep-set jawline he was, but because he had a heart of gold. From their very first date, he'd put her feelings and her happiness before his own. She couldn't have prayed for a better life companion than the man sitting across from her.

She also knew him better than anyone else did—so she waited.

Finally, he looked up and found her watching him. "What?"

She smiled. "I was wondering if you are going to tell me about the phone call or if I'll have to guess."

He shook his head and shut off the camera. "Did Alicia say something to you?"

"No."

"She's just like you, you know."

"I gather she asked the same question?"

He nodded, but unlike most times when he spoke about his daughter, a smile didn't come to his face. He sipped his wine, set the glass down, then sighed.

"The call was from Ted Baker."

"Oh?"

His eyes remained focused on his wineglass, avoiding her stare. A bad sign.

"He wanted me to know they believe the Mardi Gras killer has returned."

Air rushed from her lungs as if she'd been punched. The news she'd hoped never to hear had arrived. The Mardi Gras Killer had taken an awful toll. On the victims, of course, but also on her husband, and the whole family.

She couldn't say the killer's return was a total surprise because in truth, she was one of those who *hadn't* believed the guy was done—call it a detective's wife's intuition.

Then Vince had said he was going to retire. When she'd asked him why, he'd insisted the killer was gone, and it was time. She had kept her doubts to herself then—she might have to do that again.

"Are they sure?"

He nodded. "I spoke with Nikki."

The next question seemed as obvious as the answer. She asked anyway.

"Why did Ted want you to know?"

Vince's gaze finally came up to meet hers. "He wants me to come back."

Her throat tightened, and the room spun. She lifted her wine for a sip and hoped Vince didn't notice her hand shaking.

"What did you tell him?"

"I told him I had to talk to you."

The next question did not have an obvious answer, and she only managed to ask by sheer force of will.

"What do *you* want to do?"

He hesitated, still staring at her, searching her face. "I don't know."

Not the answer she expected. Her surprise must have shown.

He nodded slightly. "I know you expected me to say I have to go back, or I want to go back…"

That was true. "But?"

He shrugged. "But I'm not sure."

Vince rarely surprised her anymore, but she had to admit he'd caught her off guard this time. His reluctance to rush back in was unexpected. Then again, maybe she wasn't being fair to him. He had always put her first, and it appeared he was doing so again.

Suddenly, *she* wasn't certain what *she* wanted. Up until this night, she had been fixated on what Vince would do if this situation arose and had spent little time analyzing how she felt.

"Why?"

He raised an eyebrow. "Why am I unsure?"

She nodded.

He sighed. "I guess because of you and the girls. The last six months have been some of the best we've ever had as a family. I don't want to ruin that."

Rose swallowed hard and fought back the tears threatening to overflow. At this very moment, she loved this man more than she ever had.

"Vince, I know what it would mean if you could catch this guy."

He cocked his head to one side and studied her.

"I won't deny it plays a part in my thought processes, but if I'm honest, so does the chance I don't catch him."

Self-doubt was not something she saw from her husband very often.

"You can only do your best, just as you always have."

"Sure, but part of me worries I won't catch him, and then I'll have opened up old wounds for nothing."

There was a pause in the conversation, and neither seemed to know what to say next.

She broke the silence first. "I think you have to go back."

She was more surprised by the statement than he was, her words seeming to come from another person.

He stared at her with a mixture of shock and bewilderment etched on his face. "Why do you say that?"

A fierce resolve welled up inside her. "Because it's not about you, and it's not about me. It's about those women. The ones who are going to die if someone doesn't stop that animal."

His forehead creased, uncertainty oozing from every pore. "What if I can't?"

She stood and came around the table. Bending down, she kissed his forehead. "You're the only one who can."

NEW ORLEANS HOMICIDE

<u>Monday, January 29</u>

Home of Vincent and Rose Wills
Memphis Street
Lakeview Neighborhood
North New Orleans
6:25 a.m.

Rose was downstairs cleaning up after breakfast as Vince finished getting ready. He tucked his Glock G19 into the shoulder holster, put his badge case into his pocket, and pulled on his suit coat, then studied himself in the mirror. What he had once worn like a second skin now felt like the clothes of a different time, another era in his life, and the discomfort surprised him.

Sunlight came through the window and glinted off his most-prized commendation—a lapel pin.

In the aftermath of Hurricane Katrina, more than two hundred officers were accused of abandoning their posts. A tribunal reviewed each case, and roughly eighty-five percent were ultimately terminated.

Those who did their job, who put their pledge before their own safety and helped bring order back to a broken city, received the special pin. A gold crescent, centered by a gold star, emblazoned by a red weather symbol of a hurricane. It had been awarded to officers who did their job through the worst crisis New Orleans had ever faced.

Rose appeared behind him, looking over his shoulder, and examining him with a prejudicial eye. "You look good."

31

He smiled. "Thank you, but you're biased."

"Maybe, but I'm still a woman."

He turned and kissed her cheek. "Indeed you are, and a beautiful one, at that."

"Now who's biased?"

"And correct, I might add."

She smiled, but it was a smile tinged with worry. She reached up and straightened his Katrina pin. "I was so afraid for you during that time."

He nodded but didn't say anything.

"I'm worried about you now, too."

He reached out and took her in his arms. She disappeared inside his bear hug, but her arms came around him also, and they held each other for a long time. Eventually, she pushed back from him.

"Don't you have somewhere to be, Detective Wills?"

"Yes, ma'am, I do."

"Then you better get a move on."

"Yes, ma'am."

He moved past her, went to the bedroom door, then turned back. In the best McArthur imitation he could muster, he saluted. "I shall return."

She laughed then pointed at the door. "Get out of here!"

Conference Room
Major Crimes Division
Mid-City
7:45 a.m.

The Criminal Investigations building on South Broad Avenue was five stories tall, and the gray concrete façade served the purpose of making the structure blend in with all the other office buildings downtown, despite the dark subject matter of the work inside its walls. The Criminal Investigations Division was divided up into five sections—Homicide, Special Victims Section, Property Crimes, Juvenile Crimes, and the District Attorney's Office.

Vince pulled around to the back of the building, and whether by luck or providence, found his favorite old spot unoccupied. He parked and locked up before ascending to the third floor. His heart pounded as he waited for the elevator doors to open. When they did, he found himself looking at a virtually empty squad room. Just one detective, who Vince didn't recognize, tapped away on his keyboard.

He crossed the room to where his old desk had been. The nameplate now said *Detective Nikki Santiago*. He smiled to himself. There was no one he would prefer to have taken his place.

"Vince!"

He turned to see Ted Baker coming toward him.

"Morning, Lieutenant."

"Man, you're a sight for sore eyes. You just get here?"

"Yeah."

"Good. Follow me."

Vince trailed his boss into the lieutenant's office. Baker pointed at a chair. "Sit. You want a cup of coffee?"

"Sounds good."

Ted poured a cup and handed it to him then topped off his own mug before sitting down behind the desk. He rocked back in his chair and sipped his coffee. Several minutes passed while his friend studied him. Eventually, Baker set down his mug.

"You look good, Vince. Retirement agrees with you."

Vince nodded. "I must admit, it's been better than I expected."

Ted's smile evaporated. "I'm sorry about calling you like this."

"Don't be. I'm glad you did."

That wasn't completely true, but during the night, the adrenaline surge brought on by the thought of seeking a killer had returned to him. By the time he arrived at the precinct, he was ready to get to work.

Ted nodded toward the door. "Nikki is in the conference room, getting things set up. She was here late last night and early this morning so you could hit the ground running."

"You want me to use the conference room as an office?"

"Yes. Last night, after you called me, I talked again with Chief Jacobs. He said you have anything you need at your disposal."

"I appreciate that."

Baker rocked forward. "If you're ready, we can get you started."

Vince drained his paper cup and tossed it toward the garbage can in the corner. "I'm ready."

They left the office and went down a short hallway to the conference room. Ted pushed open the door then stepped back to let Vince go in first. The large table was covered in boxes, some of them stacked three high. At the far end of the room, a whiteboard had pictures taped to it with names written under them. Vince knew them all by heart.

Below the names were dates, which began at the ten-year anniversary of Katrina and moved forward to early March of last year. Eight photos in all. Off to one side of the board, was written *January 28*. Once they identified their newest victim, they'd put her photo in the blank space beneath the date.

Baker was scanning the room.

"Santiago?"

Brown hair bobbed up from behind a three-box stack. "Sir?"

"Oh, there you are. I brought you something."

Her brown eyes settled on Vince, and her face lit up. "Vince!"

She vaulted from her chair and came around the desk, wrapping him in a hug. Vince found himself caught off guard by the greeting, and he stared at her with surprise. She must have realized her fervor because she blushed slightly then regathered her composure.

"Good to see you, Vince."

He smiled broadly. "Good to see you, Nikki. How you been?"

"You'd have to ask the lieutenant."

Baker laughed. "She's doing a bang-up job, but this is a special case. Vince, let me know if there's anything you need."

"Thank you, sir."

The lieutenant left, and the door closed. Vince removed his coat and draped it over a chair. Nikki returned to her seat as he went to the pinned-up photos. He studied them briefly, then tapped the vacant spot.

"Still no identity?"

"Not yet. The morgue is taking her prints as part of the autopsy."

"When is that?"

"It's going on now."

"Good." He went over to where she sat. "What are you working on?"

"I'm looking through missing persons reports. I was hoping to find a match to our vic."

"Any luck?"

"Not so far."

Her cell phone rang. She snatched it up. "This is Santiago."

Vince went to the opposite side of the table and sat down, extracting his notepad from his jacket. Nikki was listening and nodding. She grabbed a piece of paper and wrote something down.

"Okay, thanks, Chris."

She hung up. "That was Chris Nagle. It turns out our victim had worked at a daycare and had been fingerprinted. He gave me the ID."

"Great. Who?"

"Her name is Callie Pearson. The address is in Kenner."

"That's only a half-hour away." He glanced at the wall clock. "Should we start there?"

"Sounds good to me."

Vince stood. "I'll drive."

Home of Callie Pearson
Chateau Rothchild Drive
Kenner, Louisiana
9:25 a.m.

The sixth-largest city in Louisiana, Kenner butts up against the west edge of Metairie and Greater New Orleans. Home to Louis Armstrong International Airport, Kenner was spared the worst of Katrina's flooding.

The Pearson home was located on a quiet side street dotted with mostly two-story, brick homes and immaculately groomed yards. The address Vince parked in front of was a single-story ranch with a covered porch running across the front. A landscape company was just packing up to leave after mowing.

Nikki double-checked the address. "This is it. Nice place."

"Yeah. I need to get the landscaper's card. My yard never looks like this when I'm done."

They got out of the car and followed the cement walkway up to the front door. The sun was warming the day nicely, and a pleasant breeze blew across the covered porch. Vince rang the doorbell.

In moments, a man appeared, wearing khaki shorts and a Saints football jersey. He swung the door wide. "Can I help you?"

Vince had his badge out.

"I'm Detective Wills. This is my partner, Detective Santiago. We're with the New Orleans PD."

Concern spread across the man's face. "I'm Andy Pearson. Is this about Callie?"

"Yes, sir."

"Did you find her?"

Vince glanced at Nikki, whose confused expression matched his own. Vince put away his badge.

"May we come in, sir?"

"Yes, of course."

Pearson held the door open for Vince and Nikki to enter, then shut it behind them.

"Follow me."

Nikki tailed Pearson down a short hallway, and Vince brought up the rear. The décor was modest, but like the yard outside, the home was clean and well-kept. They came out into a small kitchen with gray cabinets, black granite countertops, and stainless appliances. Vince had seen similar designs in magazines. He liked the style.

Pearson gestured toward the round glass table with four chairs. "Would you like to sit down?"

Vince remained standing, but Nikki accepted the offer. Pearson lowered himself into a seat across from her as Nikki looked up at Vince. He gave her a quick nod. When she turned back to Pearson, he was staring at her intently.

"You said you had news about Callie."

Nikki nodded. "Yes, sir. I'm afraid I have some bad news."

Right in front of him, Vince watched a man age ten years. His cheeks seemed to hollow out, his shoulders sagged, and he let out a small moan. "Oh… No."

Though he couldn't imagine going through it, Vince could understand. If something happened to either of his girls, he'd want to roll up into a ball and die.

Nikki reached out and touched the man's hand. "I'm very sorry."

He nodded then abruptly stood and went to the counter. He grabbed a hand towel and wiped at his face. The towel was insufficient for Andy Pearson's flood of tears.

After several minutes of no one speaking, an eternity to Vince as he watched the man's pain, Pearson came back to the table and sat down. He was pale, and his voice had lost its strength.

"What happened to her?"

Nikki's own voice softened. "We believe she was taken hostage and then murdered."

Inside, Vince cringed. The death of a loved one was traumatic, but invariably, finding out their family member had been murdered magnified the shock tenfold. The news seemed to have a devastating impact on Andy Pearson. Pain mixed with disbelief contorted his face.

"Murdered?" His gaze came up to Vince. "Who would want to kill my Callie?"

Vince shook his head. "Right now, we don't know, sir. We're hoping you can help us with that."

"I'm not sure how."

Vince took out his notepad. "You seemed to know your daughter was missing. Had you been trying to reach her?"

Pearson stared at the damp towel as he talked. "I'm an airline pilot, and I'd been out of town for five days, flying a European leg. When I got into town yesterday, I called Callie to let her know I was back. I got her voicemail."

Vince looked up from his notetaking. "Is that your regular routine?"

"Yeah. Anyway, she wasn't here when I got home, and after not being able to get hold of her again this morning, I called Kenner police."

"You were worried immediately?"

"Yes. Callie goes…was going to Tulane. She lived here with me, and she is always around, but it appeared she hadn't been home in days. The mailbox was full."

Vince was intrigued by the mail.

"Are you married, Mr. Pearson?"

"Divorced. My ex-wife lives in San Diego."

"We'll need her contact information. Do you know the last day Callie picked up the mail?"

"I can only guess. I'd say three or four days before."

"What about the newspaper? Do you get it delivered?"

"No. I'm not here enough."

"What about a car? Did Callie own a vehicle?"

"Yes. A blue VW, and it was gone. I gave the information to the officer from the Kenner PD."

"Okay. We can check on that with them. Did she have any friends we should speak with?"

Pearson nodded. "Brandi Cole. She goes to Tulane as well, and she is…was my daughter's best friend. I called her when I couldn't get hold of Callie, but I got Brandi's voicemail, too. She hasn't called me back."

Vince stopped writing and stared at Nikki. Did their killer have Miss Cole? Apparently, the chilling thought had crossed his partner's mind as well. Her eyes flared as her brain considered the possibility.

He turned back to Pearson. "Brandy Cole, you said?"

"Yes. I believe she spells her name with an i."

"B-r-a-n-d-i?"

Pearson nodded.

"Do you have a number for Miss Cole?"

Pearson took his phone out of his pocket and read off a number. Vince wrote it down then put his notepad away. "Thank you for your time, Mr. Pearson. I'm very sorry for your loss."

Nikki stood and handed a card to Pearson. "Sir, they'll need to speak to you at the coroner's office."

He stared at the card. "Why?"

"I'm afraid they'll need a formal identification."

His gaze came up to meet hers. The prospect clearly shook him. "Uh…okay."

"We'll let ourselves out."

Vince led the way, and after shutting the door behind them, he paused on the covered porch. Punching Brandi Cole's number into his phone, he waited. The call went straight to voicemail.

"This is Brandi. Leave a message, and hopefully, I'll remember to call you back. Just kidding. Wait for the beep."

"Miss Cole, this is Detective Wills with the New Orleans PD. Please call me as soon as you get this. It is very urgent."

He left his number and hung up.

Nikki was watching him. "What next?"

"Let's run by Kenner PD and let them know what we found."

NEW ORLEANS HOMICIDE

Kenner Police Department
Veterans Memorial Boulevard
Kenner, Louisiana
10:35 a.m.

The Kenner police headquarters was a four-story building of red-brick and white cement, which gave the impression of a fortified library. Nikki had called ahead, and they were met at the side entrance by a Sergeant Samuel Brown.

"Good Morning, Detectives."

They shook the large man's hand, which swallowed even Vince's big meat hook. Nikki followed Brown inside.

Vince brought up the rear. "Thanks for meeting with us."

"No problem. I took the missing person report on Miss Pearson…"

He opened a door into a small conference room. "I was glad to hear you had news."

Vince and Nikki filed past him and sat down at a square table. Brown closed the door then leaned against it, his arms crossed, waiting. He reminded Vince of an oversized bar bouncer, displeased with the ID given him, and glaring down from behind bulging eyelids.

Nikki cleared her throat. "Callie Pearson's body was found yesterday."

The imposing form of Samuel Brown seemed to shrink in half. He pulled out a chair and dropped heavily into it.

"Aww, that sucks. Where?"

"Off Old Gentilly Road in Venetian Isles."

"Murdered?"

Nikki nodded. "We're still waiting on autopsy."

Brown took out a notepad, which disappeared in his huge mitt, making it look as if he was reading something written on his palm.

"I'll need to call the father."

Vince shook his head. "We just came from there."

Brown raised an eyebrow. 'Oh. Sorry you had to do that."

Vince liked the big sergeant, who, despite his size—or perhaps because of it—seemed to have a big heart. Vince took out his own notepad.

"Did you speak to anyone in your investigation?"

"I checked with her teachers, and she had been in class on the previous Thursday but missed class on Friday. I also called Miss Pearson's best friend."

"Brandi Cole?"

"Yes. I got her voicemail, and she hasn't returned my call."

Vince and Nikki exchanged worried looks. Brown noticed.

"You can't get her either?"

Vince shook his head. "Not yet."

The big sergeant sighed. "That's concerning."

"That's our take, as well. Did you put out a BOLO on Miss Pearson's car?"

"Sure, but no result yet."

"Can I get the plate number and description?"

Brown read it off from his palm.

Vince made a note then passed a card to Brown. "Call us if you get a hit on the BOLO?"

"You'll be the first. Where's the body?"

"Coroner's office."

"Okay. I'll call there, then close out my file."

Vince stood, happy not to have had to reveal the cause of death and hoping to keep it that way.

"Thanks for your help."

"Anytime."

Back outside, Vince and Nikki climbed into his car, which had grown uncomfortably warm inside from the bright sun. He started the engine and rolled down his window.

"Let's go back to the precinct. I still need to review the files."

"Grab some lunch on the way?"

He glanced at his phone. "It's only eleven-fifteen. I'm not hungry yet."

She grinned. "Are you sure? I was thinking M & J's."

"Oh! Why didn't you say so? I'm starving."

She laughed and rolled her eyes. "That's what I thought."

M & J Soul Food
Lake Forest Boulevard
East New Orleans
12:15 p.m.

Just ten minutes from the precinct, M & J Soul Food was a popular lunch spot for officers and detectives alike. Situated in an L-shaped strip mall, the place had a Mom-and-Pop-diner atmosphere, and the food was as close to home cooked as anything Vince had eaten outside his wife's kitchen.

44

Daily specials included smothered chicken necks, white beans and rice, fried catfish, and Vince's favorite, fried chicken wings. The sign on the menu read *Food for the Soul.* They wouldn't get any argument from him.

He and Nikki sat at a pub table in the corner, directly under the television. Ceiling fans turned lazily overhead as folks munched on their food, the small dining room buzzing with conversation in between bites. Vince and Nikki nursed big glasses of sweet tea while they waited on their orders.

Nikki was using her straw to poke at the ice cubes in her glass. "You didn't expect the return, did you?"

He shook his head. "I felt you were ready."

Her smile was subdued. "I meant the killer's return."

Vince sipped his tea. Truth was, he'd never really been certain. When no third body showed up by the cut-off, it broke the pattern established over the previous three years. That pattern, three dead women between the start of Mardi Gras and Fat Tuesday, had been precise and consistent until last March.

Experience told him that when a pattern was broken, something had happened to the killer. A sociopath such as their guy was driven, in fact survived, by his routine. A leopard doesn't change its spots.

He shrugged. "I wasn't sure, I guess."

"But you retired anyway."

"Yeah. But more goes into the decision than just the one case."

Her eyes held his, searching him. "I can see that, but it must have been hard."

"Hard?"

"To leave such a big case unsolved."

It had been, of course, but every detective had unsolved cases. Vince hoped the guy was dead, or at the very least, serving a long prison sentence. But at a minimum, he'd felt the guy had left the area.

But maybe, he'd always known the killer would be back, but wasn't sure he could face the challenge any longer—that he didn't have what it took to catch the guy.

"Every detective has unsolved cases that bother them. At some point, you have to say you did your best and let it go. If you don't, it'll swallow you whole."

She nodded, but their food arrived, so the conversation lagged.

Vince's wings were surrounded by an oversized portion of candied yams. Nikki had opted for the red beans and rice, with a green salad. They dug in and ate in silence. Twenty minutes later, their plates had been cleared, they'd each received a to-go cup of tea, and they were back out in the car.

Vince drove out of the parking lot, letting a low moan escape as he joined the traffic on Lake Forest Boulevard. "Wow. That was good."

Nikki laughed. "How long has it been?"

"Too long. I think I had lunch with the lieutenant there about a week after I retired. I haven't been back since."

"They probably noticed the slump in sales."

He scowled at her. "Watch it, you. I still out-rank your butt!"

She grinned. "You don't scare me. I'll tell Rose you ordered real sweet tea and not the diet kind."

"You wouldn't!"

"Oh, I would."

"You're a sneaky detective, Santiago."

Her face softened. "I learned from the best."

The double-meaning didn't escape him, and he was touched. "Thanks."

He parked, and they took the elevator up to the third floor.

Nikki headed toward the conference room while Vince dumped the balance of his sweet tea and switched to coffee. He went into the conference room to find Nikki waiting by the white board, staring at some writing. She had one arm crossed in front of her, supporting her other arm that was propping up her chin.

He closed the door and sat down. "What are you looking at?"

"I started thinking about each of our victims. What they have in common with our latest victim."

"I suspect there are several things."

"Sure, but the Tulane connection between Callie Pearson and Brandi Cole got me thinking. They're all enrolled in a local college."

Vince had noticed it before but had not been able to determine how it might tie them to their killer.

"Sure, so?"

"So, who had access to that many college woman without standing out?"

"I imagine the list is quite long."

"I'll write, and you suggest."

"Okay." Vince leaned back, laced his fingers behind his head, and closed his eyes. "Fellow students, faculty members…"

"No, not faculty."

He looked at her. "Why not?"

"Because the women were from several different schools. A faculty member at Loyola isn't going to be one at Southern. Same with classmates."

"Hmmm. Then maybe people from public places where students gather?"

"Yes."

He closed his eyes again. "Bars and restaurants, concerts, sporting events, public parks and libraries…"

Nikki did her best to write quickly and keep up but finally sighed. "Stop."

"What is it?"

She tapped the list with the marker. "This isn't going to help. Look at the size of the venues. We could never track people associated with these before our killer took his next victim."

She was right, which Vince had already determined, but he wanted her to take the initiative even if it didn't pan out. Having worked this case since the beginning and without much success, he secretly hoped his partner's young mind might unlock the mystery and find a clue he'd been missing.

"You're right about one thing—the clock is ticking."

"What do you suggest?"

He pointed at her list. "Erase that."

She did then looked back at him. "Okay…

"Let's make a list of what we know for sure about each victim—just the things in common. Then we can compare it to the new autopsy results tomorrow."

She nodded, and using a green marker, she quickly jotted four things on the board in her flowing handwriting.

Cause of Death—Exsanguination.
Injuries—X-mark at wrist

Age—early to mid-twenties
No sign of sexual assault—No DNA

Vince nodded. "There's the college enrollment."
She added it.
"All were killed in the three weeks leading up to Mardi Gras."
She wrote down that connection plus another as she spoke. "Also, they were found fully dressed and positioned in the same way."
Vince grabbed a copy of the first victim's autopsy, done four years before. He scanned it then looked up. "They all had empty stomachs. They hadn't eaten in the approximately forty-eight hours prior to their death."
She made the note then turned to face him. "And their tox screens came back negative for drugs and alcohol."
"Right. Plus, they all had signs of restraints at both the knees and elbows, and a second restraint on one ankle."

Cause of Death—Exsanguination
Injuries—X-mark at wrist
Age—early to mid-twenties
No sign of sexual assault—No DNA
City college students
TOD—three weeks prior to Mardi Gras.
Same Positioning—on back with hands crossed over chest, fully clothed
Not eaten in at least forty-eight hours—stomachs empty
Tox screens clear
Ligatures—restraint marks at the knees and elbows, mark on one ankle

He scanned the list. What did it tell them? It had to connect to someone or point somewhere. What were they missing? How long could they stare at these facts and still come up empty?

Nikki capped the marker, threw it on the table, then dropped into a chair. "It's creepy."

He smiled. "Could you be more specific?"

She waved her hand at the board. "Well, look at it. He seems to be going through some sort of procedure."

Vince raised an eyebrow. "You mean like a ritual?"

"Yeah! Exactly."

"I admit the steps seem precise. But what's the purpose?"

She rotated her chair so she was now looking at him instead of the whiteboard. "The blood."

"What about the blood?"

Her expression became animated, and she tapped the table with her finger to emphasize each word.

"It's-all-about-the-blood."

"You mean for a spell or such?"

She shrugged. "Beats me, but he's doing it to get the blood for something. If we find what, we'll find him!"

Vince met his partner's gaze. He tended to agree with her about the blood's importance, and he'd considered it previously, but it was a treacherous path to venture down.

When the press first got wind that the killings were from blood loss, they had suggested the murders were evil incarnations of the *Rampart Street Murder House*.

That case, a legend in New Orleans, revolved around the murder and dismemberment of Addie Hall by her partner Zach Bowen. Eleven days later, he had jumped to his death from the eighth floor of the Omni Hotel.

In the months after Hurricane Katrina, the young couple had lived above a Voodoo shop, and their deaths led to claims that black magic had been at the core of the bizarre story. Any suggestion that the Mardi Gras murders were also tied to the ancient religion would start a hysteria that might be impossible to control.

Besides, the clock was ticking, and it was too easy to get lost in stories about dark spirits and the Queen of Voodoo, Marie Laveau. It would only serve to divert focus from finding their killer.

Still, the blood had be used for something. The most disturbing part of the puzzle was where your imagination took you when you tried to guess.

He looked up at the clock. They were stuck, waiting for the autopsy report on Callie Pearson, and still hadn't heard from Brandi Cole.

Their victim's best friend being in the wind was eating at him, and he couldn't shake the feeling there was more to the unanswered calls on her voicemail. Vince took out his phone and tried Brandi Cole's number again. As soon as the voicemail started, he hung up.

"Still going to voicemail. We need to find Brandi Cole. She might be the last one who saw Callie Pearson before she was murdered."

Nikki nodded. "If Brandi is enrolled at Tulane, they should have her address."

Vince opened his phone. "I have a friend in the registrar's office."

"Perfect."

Scanning his contacts list, he found the number of his friend and pushed the call button. It rang just once.

"University Registrar. Can I help you?"

"Vicky Blunt, please."

"May I tell her who's calling?"

"Vince Wills."

"Please hold."

Vicky Blunt had done the paperwork to get Alicia enrolled then steered her around the various pitfalls of financial aid. Since that time, whenever Vince needed some info on the university, the registrar was his first call.

"Vince! Nice to hear from you."

"Hey, Vicky. How are you?"

"Good. Busy, but good. How is Alicia doing? I haven't spoken to her in a while."

"She claims all is going well. Of course, if you really want to know, you have to ask Rose. Those two talk just about every other day."

"Has Rose tired of you being around all the time?"

Vince laughed. "Not yet, besides, I'm back at work for a little while."

"Oh? Why?"

"I'd rather not go into it right now, but I was hoping you could help me with something."

"If I can. What do you need?"

"I'm looking for one of your students. Her name is Brandi—with an i—Cole. I'm needing an address."

Vicky fell silent, and the sound of tapping computer keys came over the phone line. After just a minute, she had the information.

"She's registered at Deming Pavilion."

Vince was familiar with the place—an apartment complex rather than an official Tulane residence hall.

"Do you have a room number?"

"311."

"Thanks, Vicky."

"Anytime. Say hi to Rose for me."

"Will do." He disconnected the call. "Brandi Cole lives at Deming."

Nikki nodded. "Let's go."

Deming Pavilion
Saratoga Street
Downtown New Orleans
3:45 p.m.

Deming Pavilion sat on the corner of Saratoga Street and Tulane Avenue. Next to the Tulane Medical Center and across the street from the New Orleans Public Library, the building was about as centrally located as dorm housing could get. It even had its own Subway restaurant.

Vince found a spot along the street and parked. Once inside the main entrance, they were directed to the building manager, a middle-aged woman with short, blond hair and bright eyes.

"May I help you?"

Vince showed his badge. "I'm Detective Wills, and this is Detective Santiago. We're with the New Orleans PD."

She smiled warmly. "I'm Diana Horn. What brings you to Deming?"

She was not the stern, matronly type Vince remembered from his college dorm experience. If she was concerned by their presence, he couldn't tell.

"We're trying to reach one of your tenants. A Brandi Cole."

Miss Horn swiveled her chair to one side and opened a file cabinet without getting up. Her fingers walked along folder tabs until she came to what she sought.

"Here it is. Brandi Cole. Junior. This is her second year with us."

"We understood she was in room 311."

She swiveled back with the folder "That's correct. It's a large studio."

"We intend to knock, but if we get no answer, we would like to gain access to the apartment."

Miss Horn looked at Nikki then back at Vince. "Why?"

"She's a possible witness."

The manager closed the folder. "I don't usually enter my tenant's units without good cause."

Vince was about to explain when Nikki interrupted.

"Is murder good cause, Miss Horn?" Nikki's tone was flat and no-nonsense

Miss Horn's bright eyes widened. "Uh...well...of course."

"We're investigating a murder, and we want to make sure Miss Cole is not also a victim."

Clearly flustered now, Diana Horn stood and grabbed a key ring. "Follow me."

She scooted between the two detectives and led them off toward the elevator.

Vince grinned at his partner. "Well, that was easy."

Nikki smiled. "You just have to know how to talk to people, Vince."

He laughed. "So I see."

Apartment 311
Deming Pavilion
4:10 p.m.

Students, most carrying laptops, passed by in the hallways, paying them little attention. Memories of Vince's college years came flooding back to him as they stood outside room 311, except he'd never carried a laptop anywhere.

Three attempts to get an answer from inside the apartment failed. Finally, Vince gave the nod to open the door. Miss Horn stepped forward, unlocked it, then stepped back. A putrid odor wafted out of the apartment.

Nikki covered her nose. "That's not good."

Vince pushed the door wide and entered the small studio. Immediately to their left was a small kitchenette. Sitting on the counter was a plate that held a package. Vince shone a flashlight on it.

"There's your smell. She had apparently taken chicken out to thaw before she disappeared."

Nikki, still holding her nose, moved past Vince and turned right into the small bathroom.

"Clear."

Vince continued into the apartment, passing a small closet on the right and coming into the combination living area/bedroom. A single bed stood along the right wall, still made up and unused. A desk sat opposite the bed, and Vince's gaze went to a laptop sitting amongst the desktop clutter.

He opened the cover, and the machine came to life. The lock screen photo caught him by surprise. Two women, their hair tied up and sporting jogging outfits, smiled back at him. One was his victim, Callie Pearson.

The other was an African-American girl like Callie, but she appeared older by a few years. Her green eyes drew him in, and her smile said hello. She stood slightly behind Callie, arms draped around her neck.

Vince turned toward the door. "Miss Horn?"

The manager, who had remained outside the room, appeared. "Yes?"

He swiveled the laptop in her direction. "Is this Brandi Cole?"

"Yes."

"So, I noticed you had a key card system. She would have a card, correct?"

"Sure. Every time a tenant comes and goes, it's logged."

"What about cameras?"

"On the main entrance only."

Vince's hopes surged. "Could you look up the key card info on Brandi Cole?"

"I'll have to return to my office."

"That's fine. We'll lock up and meet you there in a few minutes."

Horn seemed skeptical then relented. "Very well."

When she was gone, Vince tried to access the laptop but had no luck. He turned to see Nikki go back into the bathroom then come out.

Concern etched her face. "No cell phone or purse."

"I can't get into her computer."

"I checked her closet—she has plenty of shoes, but I can't find a pair of running shoes."

"Why is that significant?"

Nikki pointed at the laptop. "Look at the photo. She and Callie are dressed to go jogging. If you were running, what would you take?"

Vince didn't hesitate. "Cell phone and ID."

"Right. The only set of sneakers I could find is an old pair of converse, not something you would run in."

"So, you think she went out for a run and didn't return?"

"Yes, and it's possible our victim was one of her running buddies."

"Makes sense to me. Let's see if we can confirm it with video."

He headed out the door, Nikki behind him. After locking up, they returned to the manager's office. Horn was standing at her printer. Vince tapped on the doorframe.

Horn turned and waved them in. "I'm just printing off the key card record."

She grabbed the printout from the tray and carried it over to Vince. "Here. The last swipe on Miss Cole's card was at the front door at 5:22 last Thursday afternoon."

Vince glanced at the sheet then back up at Horn. "Do you have video from then?"

Horn sat down at her desk and started punching buttons on her keyboard. After more than two minutes of searching, she turned her monitor toward Vince and Nikki.

"Here is the front door at 5:20."

Vince and Nikki both leaned on the desk, straining to get a close view of the grainy footage. The picture moved forward slowly, and they watched as students got on or off the elevator. At just past 5:21, the elevator doors opened, and two women stepped out.

Vince held up a hand. "Freeze it there!"

He and Nikki exchanged looks. His partner had been dead on. The two women were dressed in shorts, t-shirts, and running shoes. Callie carried a set of keys, and Brandi had a small pink clutch tucked under one arm.

Nikki looked at Miss Horn. "Let it roll."

The picture moved again, and they tracked people leaving the building. Nobody suspicious seemed to be following the girls.

Nikki sighed. "That's good. Can we have a copy?"

Horn nodded. "I'll have to send it when I can get a duplicate done."

"That's fine."

"Do you want to see the outside camera?"

Both detectives stared at her.

Horn squirmed slightly. "Well?"

Vince nodded. "Absolutely. I thought you only had the front door."

"Right—inside and out."

More keyboard punching produced a wide-angle picture of the sidewalk outside. This time, the picture moved forward from 5:22 and showed the two girls leaving and turning right. At the edge of the picture, they turned again, this time into the parking lot.

Forty-five seconds later, a small blue car pulled out of the lot and turned east on Saratoga Street. Nobody followed them. Vince watched the car disappear, the irony hitting him like a punch in the gut. Soon, at least one of the girls would be gone forever. The thought dragged on his heart, but the burden of not knowing what had happened to Brandi Cole was worse.

He turned to Horn. "We'll need a copy of that video as well, please."

"Sure."

"Do you have an emergency contact for Miss Cole?"

"Uh, yes." She opened the folder she had retrieved earlier. "Beverly Cole. She's listed as Brandi's mother."

"Where from?"

"Jackson, Mississippi."

Vince wrote down the name, city, and phone number. "If you hear from Miss Cole, please let us know immediately."

"I will."

He looked at Nikki, who was already moving toward the door. Vince dialed the number the manager had given him then followed his partner.

As he arrived back at their car, a recording came on the line.

"This is Beverly. Sorry I'm not available. Please leave a message."

Vince did then climbed in behind the wheel. "Voicemail at the mother's number."

Nikki checked her watch. "It's almost six."

Vince considered their options. Without a clear picture of what to do next, it seemed their best option was to call it a day and start fresh in the morning with the autopsy report.

"I guess we need to wait for the autopsy findings to decide what our next move should be."

Vince's phone rang. "Detective Wills."

"Yes, Detective, this is Sergeant Brown with the Kenner PD."

"Hello, Sergeant. What can I do for you?"

"We got a hit on the car."

Vince's gaze flicked over to his partner. "Callie Pearson's Volkswagen?"

Nikki's breathing seemed to stop as she froze, watching him.

"That's right. One of your mounted officers spotted it at City Park, not far from the New Orleans PD stables."

"Anyone around?"

"Not that I am aware of."

"Where is it exactly?"

"A small parking area off the circle just south of Couturie Forest."

Vince's mental map placed the location immediately. "I know where it is. Thanks for the call."

"Anytime."

Hanging up, he smiled at Nikki. "What I said about waiting on the autopsy for our next move...forget that."

Couturie Forest
City Park
Central New Orleans
6:45 p.m.

The 1,300-acre greenspace had been the center of New Orleanians outdoor activities since 1854, making it one of the nation's oldest city parks. It had served as the backdrop for dances, concerts, art, and even duels known as "affaires d'honneur." Attractions included the Museum of Art, a golf course, a botanical garden, and the largest collection of mature live oaks—some of them over eight hundred years old—in the world.

Beginning just ten blocks from Lake Ponchartrain, the park stretched south from Robert E. Lee Boulevard to City Park Avenue. Bordered on the east by Bayou Saint John and on the west by Orleans Avenue Canal, the huge park was a mile wide and three miles long.

The New Orleans Police stables were located just off Harrison Avenue, but Vince didn't stop. A set of police cruiser lights flashed on the other side of a small bridge near the entrance to the parking area. Vince pulled onto the swale, and Nikki and he got out.

An officer approached from where crime tape stretched across the small entrance.

"Detective Wills?"

Vince nodded.

"We were told you were on your way."

Vince gestured toward Nikki. "This is my partner, Detective Santiago."

The officer touched his cap. "Ma'am. I'm Officer Dupree. The car is this way."

Vince allowed Nikki to duck under the tape first then followed her as they tailed Dupree over to the little blue car. As the officer walked, he explained the apparent delay in calling the car's tag in.

"Three officers had reported seeing the car over the last few days, but it wasn't until one of them saw it for the second time and realized it hadn't moved that he checked the plate."

From several yards away, Vince noticed the white film of gravel dust that covered the vehicle.

"Has anyone touched the car?"

Dupree shook his head. "When the BOLO popped up, we decided to leave it alone."

Vince took out a handkerchief and tried the door. It was locked. Peering through the driver's window, he saw nothing out of the ordinary. Nikki was doing the same thing on the passenger side.

"Vince."

"Yeah?"

"I've got something over here."

He went around to the other side.

Nikki pointed. "I think that might be the one we saw Brandi carrying on the Deming video."

Vince stared down at the floorboard. A pink purse lay partially open.

"I think you're right."

"So we can assume this is where they came to run, you think?"

Vince stood and looked down the path leading away from the parking area. Couturie Forest was comprised of sixty acres of thick trees, and he'd walked the park trails many times, either alone or with Rose.

He turned to Officer Dupree. "Any other vehicles here when you called this in?"

"None."

"Okay. We need to do a search of all the forest trails. Get me as many officers from the mounted division as you can. I'll call for some patrol cruisers to help."

Dupree nodded and walked back to his car. Nikki had already pulled out her phone and was talking to dispatch. After a moment, she hung up.

"Help is coming."

"Good." He glanced at his watch. "It's going to be a long night."

****

Using flashlights and multiple officers, including a canine unit, officers searched the trails for any sign of Brandi Cole. The mounted division sent five officers and their horses, which cut the search time by hours. Each horse and rider team could do the work of a dozen officers.

They found nothing.

By ten-thirty, a frustrated Vince called off the search, and just past eleven-fifteen, the Volkswagen was towed to the forensics garage, freeing him and Nikki to head home.

Officers from the mounted division would conduct another search at daybreak, but Vince was not optimistic. His eyelids were heavy, and his body ached, but neither pained him as much as not finding Brandi Cole. He was beginning to believe she was being held by their killer. If he was right, then she—like himself—had to sense her time was running out.

Home of Vincent and Rose Wills
Memphis Street
Lakeview Neighborhood
North New Orleans
11:55 p.m.

Returning to work a case managed to rekindle many of Vince's memories. Some were positive, like the comradery of his partnership with Nikki, but many were negative. He had not missed the sheer exhaustion that came from trying to outwork, outthink, and outfox a perpetrator. Neither had he missed the routine he found himself reliving as he arrived home.

Too many nights to remember had ended with him slipping his key as silently as possible into the door, turning the lock, and trying to get inside without waking Rose, the kids, or both. Invariably, if he woke one of the girls, he would find Rose already up and shooing them back to bed. Then she'd return to bed herself and wait.

When he made it up the stairs, she would be sitting up in bed, their bathroom light on so he could see. What he never told her was how much he treasured seeing her, illuminated by the small light, waiting for him to come to bed. He'd never tired of it.

On this night, he crept into the bedroom, already aware the bathroom light was on. Her eyes glistened slightly as he came to the bed and sat next to her. The smile on her face looked forced.

"Long day?"

He nodded. "You, too?"

"Spent most of the day praying and the rest of it missing you."

He smiled wearily and laid his head on her lap. She kissed the top of his forehead and ran her fingers through his hair. He passed out with his shoes still on.

Tuesday, January 30

Lower Ninth Ward
New Orleans
5:45 a.m.

The ninth ward voting district had two areas designated by planners, the Holy Cross Neighborhoods and the Lower Ninth. Designated "lower" because of being farther down toward the mouth of the Mississippi River, the Lower Ninth has become synonymous with the devastation brought on by Hurricane Katrina.

Pictures of people dangling precariously from helicopters rising above homes with large painted letters declaring "HELP US" across their rooftops had been broadcast across the world. No area had suffered greater destruction, and no area had a longer road back than the Lower Ninth.

But it was the killer's home.

The memories of the days following the flooding were etched in his mind, and what he remembered most was the fear. Fear borne out of helplessness and despair as the flood waters rose, forcing them onto the roof, then to the very peak, so they couldn't even lie down without getting wet. He never wanted to experience that again.

Even if he tried to forget those days, the photo on his mantle prevented him from doing so. Like countless others taken during that time, it had been shot by someone looking down from a helicopter as terrified people were plucked from the devastation. The significant thing about this picture was who the people were—himself and his father.

In the picture, he peered up through pelting water droplets whipped by the chopper blades, and with Armageddon-like fear painted across his face, sought help from above. He had his arms wrapped around his father, keeping the old man steady against the down-rushing air, while his father gripped the family bible tightly in both hands.

During the entire time on the roof, his father had not stopped praying for them and for his city, even as they lifted him in the basket. New Orleans had been his father's home since he came into the world, and he'd grieved over what had happened to it.

Now, reaching over and picking up that same bible, the killer turned it over in his hands. Stained and weathered from those days and twisted from the moisture, it reminded him of the crosses he'd seen atop churches that'd been hit by a tornado. Warped, bent, but not defeated.

He flipped the bible open to his favorite passage.

"Greater love has no one than this, that he lay down his life for his friends."

His father was gone now, but that and many other scriptures taught to him by the man continued to steer the killer's life.

A noise from the back bedroom broke his concentration. He laid the bible back in its place next to the photo and went into the kitchen. From the fridge, he took out a bottle of purified water and carried it into the unlocked bedroom.

The chain around her ankle grated heavily as she recoiled against the wall.

From the far corner of the bed, she stared at him, eyes wide. "Don't hurt me!"

He tossed the bottle onto the bed and leaned against the doorframe. The small bedroom was sealed from the outside, and a single overhead bulb provided the only light. The dank air smelled of urine and body odor.

"What is it?"

"Water."

Wary and afraid, she eyed the bottle suspiciously, but her thirst soon got the better of her. She snatched it up and drained it in three gulps then retreated to the far end of the bed. He turned to go.

"Where is Callie?"

He paused but didn't look back.

"In a better place."

The sound of her sobbing followed him out the door.

Office of Orleans Parish Coroner
Earhart Boulevard
Central New Orleans
9:45 a.m.

The coroner's officer had shared an old, gray building—a perfect example of efficiency before artistry—with the emergency services department. After Katrina had decimated the structure and forced the coroner to move into a former funeral home in Central City, a new structure had been built. The new facility was state-of-the-art and light-years better.

Chris Nagle sported his standard blue scrubs as he led Vince and Nikki into his office, a neat and orderly space that, in Vince's mind, went against nature. But then again, Vince's form of organization at his desk only had three levels: The "in" box, the "out" box, and the trash can. Fortunately, he'd been blessed with partners who were able to keep the case files in better order than he ever could. Vince worked from his notepad and his memory, although the latter was becoming less reliable all the time.

Chris sat behind his desk. "So, Vince, getting up to speed yet?"

Vince groaned. "It's only been one day."

Nagle glanced at Nikki. "You running him too hard?"

Nikki laughed. "Hardly! The man refuses to go home at night. We were out searching Couturie Forest until nearly midnight."

"Midnight? You can't see anything at midnight in those woods." Nagle pointed at two chairs across from his desk. "Have a seat."

Vince accepted the offer. "It wasn't midnight! Maybe eleven."

Nikki stayed by the door. "Whatever. It was late."

The coroner raised an eyebrow. "What were you looking for?"

Vince nodded toward a file folder on the desk. "Her best friend."

Nagle picked it up. "Callie Pearson's?"

"Yeah. They were last seen together. You have Callie, but nobody has seen her friend, Brandi Cole."

Vince's ringing phone interrupted them. "Excuse me." He answered the call. "Detective Wills."

"Yes, Detective. My name is Beverly Cole. You left a message for me to call you."

"Yes, ma'am. Thanks for returning my call. It's about your daughter, Brandi."

"Is she okay?"

"Well, without sounding too alarmist, we're concerned about her whereabouts. Have you spoken with her?"

"Not since last week—Thursday, I believe. What is going on?"

"Are you familiar with your daughter's friend, Callie Pearson?"

"Of course."

Vince rubbed his eyes wearily. "I'm afraid Miss Pearson was found dead this past Sunday."

"Dead? What…what happened?"

"She was murdered."

There was a long silence on the other end, and when Beverly Cole came back on, her voice trembled.

"I tried to call Brandi when I got your message but got her voicemail. Do…is she dead, too?"

"We don't have anything to suggest that. We just want to make sure your daughter is safe. Can you think of anyone else she might contact or anyplace she might be?"

Another pause. "Not really. My husband passed away several years ago, and she's not close to anyone else in the family."

Vince realized he was holding up Chris Nagle. "Mrs. Cole, I need to go. Will you call me if you hear anything from your daughter?"

"Of course, but I'm coming down there now."

"Very well. Contact me when you arrive."

"I will."

Vince hung up. "Sorry about that, Chris."

Nagle waved a hand. "No problem at all."

Vince turned to Nikki. "Beverly Cole hasn't heard anything from her daughter since last Thursday."

NEW ORLEANS HOMICIDE

Nikki nodded. "Sounded like she's on her way here."

"That's right. Can't blame her—I would be, too."

"Definitely."

Nagle held out a folder to Vince. "This is what you're after, I assume."

Vince opened it and looked at a couple photos. The bruising around one ankle stood out.

"How about the short version?"

Nagle nodded. "Familiar story. Blood drained from X-marks at wrists, no sign of sexual assault, no DNA, ligature bruises at the elbows and knees, plus the one at the ankle."

Nikki was taking notes. "What about stomach contents?"

"None."

"So, TOD would be…"

"Late Saturday night, probably between ten and midnight."

"What about tox screen?"

"Like the others, we ran it using what we call vitreous humour."

Nikki cocked her head to one side. "Is this about you being funny again?"

Nagle laughed. "No, but coroners *are* funny people."

"Like I said before, I'll take your word for it."

"Anyway, vitreous humour is a jelly-like substance extracted from behind the eye. It's suitable for testing for all kinds of things, including drugs and alcohol."

Both Nikki and Vince groaned.

Nagle looked up. "What?"

Vince smirked. "Just the whole idea of extracting an eyeball."

"With what you guys see, pardon the pun, why does the idea of removing an eye creep you out?"

70

Vince shrugged. "It just does."

"Well, to answer your question, the screen was clear."

Vince stood. "Thanks. Anything else?"

"Afraid not."

"We'll talk to you later then."

Deanie's Seafood Restaurant
Iberville Street
French Quarter
11:10 a.m.

Vince turned down Iberville and into the multi-level parking garage. Circling upward until he reached the rooftop parking, he chose a space, and they got out. An elevator took him and Nikki down to Deanie's Seafood.

Located on the west edge of the French Quarter in a French-colonial-style building, the white structure with green doors and shutters came complete with a traditional balcony. Popular with locals and tourists alike, the restaurant's specialty was fried anything but especially seafood.

They had chosen to sit at the counter surrounding the bar, and Vince knew exactly what he wanted. "Crawfish Po-Boy sandwich with fries."

"Half or Full?"

"Full!"

Nikki was having a harder time deciding. "It all looks so good."

Vince's stomach growled loud enough to be heard across the room. "We're not going to taste any of it if you don't order."

Their server was waiting patiently for the decision. He'd known Nikki and Vince for a couple years, and Nikki's hemming and hawing was nothing new.

Finally, she closed the menu. "Shrimp Po-Boy, hold the fries."

"Half or full?"

"Just the half."

"Very well."

With their orders submitted, Vince dumped a packet of sweetener into his ice-water with lemon.

Nikki sneered. "That's not lemonade; I don't care what you say."

"Almost as good."

Their food arrived, and they ate without further conversation, each focusing on their sandwich. Eventually, all that remained were some of Vince's fries.

He groaned. "I'm stuffed. You want a fry?"

Nikki reached over and extracted two. After devouring them, she sipped her tea before looking at Vince. He could see an idea forming just by the look in her eyes—distant but flared.

"What is it, Nikki?"

"I was thinking about the last few years. This guy has been killing for what, three years before now?"

"Yeah. So?"

"Well, what we've been doing hasn't allowed us to catch him. We need to try something new."

"Okay. Such as?"

Her fingers drummed on the bar, a sure sign her adrenaline was surging. "Why don't we call a press conference and speak directly to the killer."

Their server showed up and topped off Vince's water. He tapped a package of sweetener before dumping it in.

The idea was different, in part because of the directness but also because they had tried to keep the case low profile. The mayor, and thus the chief of police, hadn't wanted a bunch of negative publicity during the premier tourist event of the year.

Only the basics had been given at press conferences in the past, with things like the fact that the victims had been drained of blood, being kept under wraps.

He stirred then sipped his water, stalling. After a moment, he sighed.

"Okay, if I agree with you—and that's a big if—what do you hope to accomplish?"

The finger drumming ceased as she concentrated. "Smoke him out. Insult him, maybe. Then see if he makes a mistake."

Vince considered it. The tactic wasn't new, and had been used before by departments around the country, but it was risky. Their killer could ramp things up and shed even more blood. Or he could not take the bait and go into hiding.

Vince continued to swizzle his lemonade-ish water, focusing on the glass rather than looking at Nikki. "How would you provoke him?"

"Well…I'm not sure."

She closed her eyes, and Vince waited. When she reopened them, her whole body seemed to vibrate. He'd seen her behave this way before, every time she came up with an idea.

"How about this? He seems to have a ritual or process that drives him. What if we mock it?"

"Mock it how?"

"Maybe suggest he's warped, and his killings serve no purpose. Maybe he'll reach out to justify himself."

Vince liked it, though he wasn't at all certain he could get the higher-ups to okay the idea.

"So, if I agree—still not saying I do—I have one condition before I'll bring the idea up to the lieutenant."

Suspicion crept into his partner's stare. "Which would be?"

"I do the news conference, and you stay in the background."

"That's two conditions."

"Okay, then let's say this. You won't speak at the news conference."

She glared at him. He waited.

She turned back to stare at her drink, and the finger-drumming restarted.

Without looking up, she asked the obvious question. "Why?"

He sighed. "It's not about whose idea the conference is—I'm glad to tell the lieutenant you suggested the direct confrontation—but…"

She turned her head to look at him. "But?"

"I won't risk putting you in danger."

Her face reflected confusion. "Danger how?"

"Look, this guy is killing women—young women. If you stand up there and challenge him, he may take it personally and come after you."

She stared at him, and he watched as she processed his words.

"But I'm not attending a local university."

"True, but if we jerk his chain, he might change his M.O."

"Okay, let's say you're right; we could use that to catch him."

Adamant, Vince shook his head. "Not a chance. Running a short-term sting with you as bait is one thing, but we can't watch you all the time."

She rotated to face him, resolve in her eyes. "I can take care of myself."

"I'm not saying you can't, but that's my condition."

He met her stare with one of his own and did his best to convey the conviction he felt. He would not risk her safety, regardless of what case they were working.

After a tense moment, her glare softened. "Fine."

"Fine?"

"I agree not to speak at the press conference."

"Good."

"So you'll propose it today?"

"I will. What's more, I'll pick up your lunch tab."

She smiled. "Oh, now you tell me! I would have had lobster if I'd known you were going to do that."

He raised an eyebrow. "Of course, you would have. Momma didn't raise no fool!"

NEW ORLEANS HOMICIDE

Major Crimes Division
715 South Broad Avenue
Mid-City
1:10 p.m.

When they arrived back at the precinct, Vince's first order of business was to check on the search for Brandi Cole. Officers from the mounted division had planned on giving the Couturie Forest another sweep in daylight and should have been done by now. He'd expected to hear something already.

Dropping into a chair in the conference room, he picked up the phone to dial.

Nikki spotted a piece of paper on the table and picked it up. "They didn't find anything new at Couturie."

Vince put down the receiver. "That's disappointing."

She tossed the paper into the trash. "Very."

Vince got up and checked Lieutenant Baker's door. It was closed.

He glanced at Nikki. "I'll be back in a moment."

He crossed to the lieutenant's office and tapped on the door.

A brief hesitation was followed by a loud, "Come!"

Vince opened the door and stuck his head inside the room.

Baker was holding his hand over the phone. "What is it, Vince?"

"I need a few moments of your time."

"Of course. Give me five minutes to finish this call, and we'll talk."

"Okay. In the conference room?"

"Sure."

Vince returned to the conference room to find Nikki on the phone. He retook his chair and waited. She jotted something on a pad then hung up.

"That was forensics. Callie Pearson's VW was clean. It had been wiped down, and the lab didn't even find Callie or Brandi's prints."

"Interesting."

"How so?"

"Well, why wipe down a vehicle if you were never in it?"

"You think our guy used the car?"

Vince ran his hand through his hair, which he suspected was turning grayer with every passing hour.

"Possibly. If he took both girls at once, then the car would be the best method. Surprise them while they're still inside, probably with a weapon, then have Callie drive them to wherever it is he's keeping them."

"Then he returns the car and picks his up?"

"Makes sense. Both girls were athletic, and it's unlikely he'd gain control over both on a trail, right?"

"Yeah. So how does that help us?"

Vince sighed. "I don't know."

Ted Baker came into the room, carrying a cup of coffee. He closed the door behind him then took a chair at the far end of the table.

"Where are we on things?"

Vince shrugged. "We believe we've identified who the next victim will be."

Baker's eyes lit up. "That's great. Can we trap our killer?"

"No, sir. We know who she is because we think he already has her."

Baker appeared to choke on his coffee. He set down the mug.

"Why do you say that?"

"We've discovered that our first victim was with a friend. That friend—Brandi Cole—went missing the same time Callie Pearson did."

"So you think he is holding her until when?"

"Whenever he decides to kill her."

Baker looked over at Nikki, as if seeking confirmation. Her face apparently gave him his answer.

He picked up his coffee mug and drained it then turned back to Vince.

"Is that what you wanted to see me about?"

Vince shook his head. "Santiago had an idea, and I think it's worth a shot."

Baker regarded his female detective. "Okay?"

Nikki looked at Vince uncertainly. He gestured for her to go ahead.

"Uh…well…I suggested to Vince that we hold a press conference."

Baker nodded. "Why?"

Nikki hesitated again.

Vince jumped in. "The idea was to confront our killer through the media. Call him out, get under his skin, and try to get him to make a mistake."

Baker listened but his gaze went to the ceiling. "How?"

Nikki found her voice. "His ritual. Mock it or demean it somehow."

Baker was still staring off into space, as if listening to a distant voice. Vince suspected that voice might be the chief or the mayor, maybe both.

Baker cleared his throat. "You realize Fat Tuesday is just two weeks away."

Vince nodded. "Yes, sir. But that is two more lives lost if our killer sticks to his pattern, and then we have the same problem next year."

"What kind of information do you want to release that isn't already out there?"

"That the bodies are being drained of blood."

Baker stared at him as if he'd lost his mind. "Do you have any idea the level of hysteria that could cause?"

"Of course. But perhaps we can word it in a way that attacks him without being over-descriptive to the public."

"How would you do that?"

Vince shrugged. "We haven't gotten that far yet."

Baker shook his head. "No way, Vince. The chief won't go for it because the mayor won't go for it."

"Will the idea cause any more hysteria than another dead college student."

Baker's stare locked on Vince. "I don't think it's a wise plan, and I won't bring it to the chief."

Vince returned the stare, his insides churning with frustration and anger.

"Look, Ted, you asked me to come back and run this investigation…"

"I know that."

"Well, I think this is our best shot to smoke this guy out. If you won't back me on it, then you can get someone else to work this case. I'm done!"

Vince wasn't bluffing. He wouldn't have more bodies laid at his feet because politics got in the way. He had seen enough of that in his career, and he wouldn't tolerate it any longer.

At first, Baker didn't flinch. But soon, his glare softened. "You're right. You stepped back into this mess, and the least I can do is back you."

"Thank you."

"But first, I want you to put together notes on what you plan to say and how you'll say it. I'll take them with me to the chief."

Vince nodded. "Give us an hour."

Baker stood. "Take two. I'm already scheduled to meet Jacobs at four."

"Yes, sir."

The lieutenant rose and left the room, closing the door behind him.

Nikki was staring at Vince, her head cocked to one side. He sensed she wanted to ask if he'd meant it, but she knew the answer—he never made idle threats.

Instead, she reached across for her pad. "Where do we start?"

An hour and half later, they had their press conference planned out. Vince delivered the notes to Baker then returned to the conference room. He forced a wry smile.

"Now, we wait."

City Hall
1300 Perdido Street
Downtown New Orleans
4:10 p.m.

Ted Baker parked and bolted from his car. When he'd phoned Chief Jacobs and briefed him on what his detectives wanted to do, Jacobs had moved the meeting to the mayor's office. The change meant Baker was running late, not something you ever wanted to do with Mayor Sheila Curry, and especially not when you were bringing news she wasn't going to like in the first place.

A long, concrete stairway led up to the ten-story, cement and blue-glass structure. He took it two steps at a time. As city halls went, this one was fairly ordinary with nothing other than the huge, square letters that spelled out the words "city hall" running across the façade at the top to set it apart from the other office buildings around it.

He ignored the elevator and double-jumped the stairs up to the third floor. When he came out into the hallway, sucking air from the effort, Jacobs was waiting for him.

"Hey, Chief. Sorry I'm late."

Jacobs shook his head. "Don't worry about it. We're waiting for a phone conference to end."

Ted bent over at the waist. "Good. I need to catch my breath."

Jacobs smiled. "I understand; a desk job will kill you. Do you have the notes?"

Without straightening up, Ted handed the manila folder containing the three-page statement to his boss. Jacobs, not quite six feet tall, was still in decent shape. His biceps complained at the restriction of his button-down shirt, and his chest stuck out just as far as his stomach, no small feat for a man who sat behind a desk most of the time. His once black hair had turned completely gray, but he had so far avoided the receding hairline of most men his age, which contributed to making him look younger than his fifty-one years.

Jacobs opened the folder and scanned the contents. Ted watched as his boss read, then glanced up at Ted, then read some more. Jacobs repeated this several times before eventually closing the folder and letting out a sigh.

"Curry is gonna freak."

Ted stood up. "We have to sell her, Cap."

Jacobs' expression turned pained. "You mean *I* have to."

Ted raised an eyebrow. "Alone?"

"Yeah. You get to wait outside."

Ted had mixed feelings about this news. The meeting would be no tea party, and waiting outside was okay with him, but he'd given Vince his word. Still, if anybody was capable of delivering an unpopular idea, it was Jacobs. He'd risen through the department ranks primarily through his time at Internal Affairs, including being involved with the Post-Katrina investigations.

The double-wooden doors opened, and the mayor's receptionist appeared. "The mayor is ready for you, Chief Jacobs."

Jacobs nodded and turned to Ted. "Wish me luck."

"Chief?"

Jacobs paused. "Yeah?"

"Vince Wills believes in this, and I believe in Vince…"

Jacobs winked at him. "Don't worry. I'm in your corner on this one, too."

Ted nodded and watched his chief disappear through the doors. He felt a little like King Darius watching Daniel enter the lion's den. If only Jacobs' encounter with the mayor would turn out as well.

Major Crimes Division
715 South Broad Avenue
Mid-City
5:30 p.m.

Vince and Nikki took turns pacing. One would walk the floor from one end of the squad room to the other while their counterpart stared at the clock. It had been well over an hour since the lieutenant had called and told them Jacobs had gone in alone.

Vince was on the return leg of his recent trek around the room when he saw Nikki nod toward the elevator. "He's back."

Vince turned just as Baker passed by him.

"My office," the lieutenant said.

Vince exchanged looks with Nikki, and she stood and joined him in following the lieutenant. When all three were inside the office, Baker shut the door and went behind his desk. He dropped heavily into his chair then tossed the folder onto his desk.

"The mayor made a few changes, but you got your green light."

Vince exhaled loudly. "Sweet!"

Nikki grabbed the folder and scanned the changes.

Vince sat opposite his boss. "Did Jacobs say how the meeting went?"

Ted grinned. "He said it was like being mauled by an angry housecat."

Vince laughed, partly from the description and partly from relief.

Nikki handed the folder to him. "I only see one major change."

"What's that?"

"She changed the term 'intentional blood-letting' to 'exsanguination'."

"I can live with that." Vince closed the folder. "When can we schedule the news conference?"

Ted shrugged. "Whenever you want."

Vince looked back at Nikki. "What do you think?"

"Tomorrow morning, say ten?"

"Works for me. Ted?"

Another shrug. "I'll let the chief know."

Vince stood and extended his hand. "Thanks."

Ted shook with him. "You're welcome. Let's hope it pays off."

"Amen to that!"

When they got back to their desks, Nikki picked up her phone. "I'm gonna call Beverly Cole."

"You want to see if she's made it into town?"

"Yeah. Perhaps we can have her at the press conference."

Vince nodded. "I like it."

She dialed the phone while he sat down to review the notes. As Nikki had said, the changes were all minor except for the one, which was a better result than he'd thought possible.

Nikki hung up and smiled. "She's at the Days Inn off I-10. She didn't sound thrilled with the idea but said she would be here in the morning."

"Perfect. Let's make the changes to our statement, then call it a night."

Wednesday, January 31

Media Room
Major Crimes Division
715 South Broad Avenue
Mid-City
9:50 a.m.

Vince stuck his head through the door to judge the size of the media turnout. Perhaps it shouldn't have, but the packed room surprised him. Though not large, the space along the bare white walls and gray folding chairs of the precinct media room were rarely full, but on this day, the room's capacity seemed to be stretched to the maximum.

Most press conferences would draw the standard crowd—beat reporters for newspapers in the city, *The Advocate, Times-Picayune,* and *Tribune,* as well as the local TV affiliates—but he spied several reporters he rarely saw. Even the smaller publications such as *The Louisiana Weekly* had sent a reporter, who was flanked by a *Telemundo* representative on one side, and a FOX News radio analyst on the other.

The small group of young folks gathered near the back was of particular interest. Their press passes identified them as college students with the *Loyola Maroon,* the *Tulane Hullabaloo,* and the University of New Orleans paper, *Driftwood.* They could connect with one of the groups he and Nikki most wanted to reach—college-age women.

He ducked back into the ready room just off the stage, slightly more nervous than before. He'd done many press conferences in his career, and for the most part, they were dull affairs. This meeting would not be one of those.

Nikki had been looking over his shoulder. "Big turnout."

He nodded. "Did you notice the college press at the back?"

"I did. I'm glad to see them."

"Me too. Any word from Beverly Cole?"

"The lieutenant is escorting her up now."

Vince checked the wall clock. 9:53. "Jacobs should be here anytime."

Nikki nodded. "What about Beverly Cole? Do you want her to speak?"

"Let's see how she's doing and then decide."

He pulled out the three sheets of paper containing their statement. Giving them a final once over, he concluded he was as ready as he would ever be.

Moments later, a woman in her mid-to-late forties was led into the room by Ted Baker. Nikki smiled and went over to her.

"Hello, Beverly. I'm Detective Santiago."

"Good morning. I'm sorry I'm late."

"No apology necessary. I want you to meet my partner, Detective Wills."

She extended a reticent hand. "Nice to meet you, Detective."

Vince wrapped his big mitt around her tiny fingers. She was ice cold. "Call me Vince, please."

She nodded. "Very well."

Vince instinctively wrapped his other hand over top his first in an effort to steady her. She glanced up at him, her lips trembling. He ruled out having her speak.

Looking directly into her eyes, he smiled. "Have you heard from your daughter?"

"No."

"Okay. We're going to get her picture out there and do our best to find her."

"What do you want me to do?"

"Nothing. You'll stand next to Lieutenant Baker and Detective Santiago at the back of the stage. I'll recognize your presence, but you don't need to speak."

She gave him a weak smile. "Good."

Vince squeezed her hand. "It'll be fine. We appreciate you being here."

"I'd do anything for Brandi."

Vince looked up at the clock. 9:59.

Chief Jacobs strode into the room and crossed to where the group stood. He nodded at Baker and Nikki, who introduced Beverly Cole.

Jacobs gave her a warm smile. "Nice to meet you." He then turned toward Vince and made eye contact. "You ready?"

"Yes, sir."

"Let's go then."

He led the way out onto the small stage and walked to the podium. Vince, followed by Beverly, Nikki, and the lieutenant, went through the door. Stopping just inside the room, they lined up with their heels teetering on the back edge of the stage. With the mother between them, Vince and Nikki crossed their hands in front of them and stared straight ahead at the far back wall.

Jacobs and Baker were both in full dress uniform, but neither Vince nor Nikki had dressed up for the occasion—a suggestion from the mayor's office—that was meant to give the appearance they'd just interrupted the detective's hard casework to be at the press conference. Vince had wondered if that meant she thought they *weren't* hard at work, but opted not to make the point.

Jacobs turned on the microphone and cleared his throat. The room fell silent.

"Ladies and Gentlemen, thank you for joining us on such short notice. In a moment, I'm going to turn the podium over to Detective Vince Wills. He'll speak about the investigation and then read a statement, after which he will answer questions." He paused and sipped a glass of water that had been pre-positioned. "But first, Mayor Curry has asked me to make one thing clear. The information you are about to receive is not meant to cause the good citizens of New Orleans an excess of concern. Our detectives are hard at work, and their only goal in giving this news conference is to seek assistance from the public. Any help is greatly appreciated, and all tips will be followed up on."

Another sip of water. Vince wondered if "water drinking pauses" was a course at some politicians' seminar. Another throat clear.

"To re-enforce our commitment to solving this case, the usual five-thousand-dollar reward for information on our tip line is being increased to ten thousand. Mayor Curry will spare no expense to find the man responsible for these heinous crimes."

Vince spotted the tightening in Nikki's jaw. She stole a glance in his direction, and he raised an eyebrow. They hadn't been told about the reward fund increase.

Vince checked the lieutenant's reaction. Nothing. Was he bluffing, or had he been kept in the dark on that, too?

Either way, the increase meant two things. First, it would certainly catch folks attention and lead to more calls, which Vince saw as a good thing. Second, a large reward would cause the phone lines to be inundated by crackpot callers sharing outlandish tips. A classic, good-with-the-bad scenario if he'd ever seen one.

Sensing his moment was near, Vince drew in a long breath and focused his thoughts. He wasn't here to speak to the media, not really, but to the killer. The message had to tweak him enough to make him reach out—at least, that was the hope.

Jacobs cleared his throat again. "I'll now turn it over to Detective Wills."

Vince stepped forward and nodded at Jacobs. Jacobs took up a position next to Baker as Vince laid his paper on the lectern. He looked up, choosing to focus on the college students at the back.

"Thank you for coming. I would like to extend a special welcome to the members of the college press who have joined us."

Many in the room turned to look at the young people, who seemed briefly embarrassed. Vince cleared his throat, caught himself, and swallowed back a sardonic chuckle. Apparently, it was catching.

"As the chief said, I'm going to read a statement, after which I will take questions. But first, some business related to the case."

He turned and gestured toward an easel standing by the side of the stage. On it were two photos—one of a blue VW and the other of Brandi Cole.

"The young woman in this photo is Brandi Cole, age twenty-three. She's a student at Tulane and we are attempting to locate her." He nodded toward the rear of the stage. "With us today is her mother, Beverly Cole, and she is asking for the help of all New Orleanians in finding her daughter."

Beverly nodded, her expression grave. He returned to the photos.

"The blue VW is the vehicle Miss Cole was last known to be in. We are asking anyone who has seen this car or spoken with Miss Cole to call the tip line. She is considered to be at risk. Copies of the photos will be provided before you leave."

Some hands shot up but he ignored them.

"At this time, I want to read the statement referenced by Chief Jacobs. Some of the information in this statement has been released before, some of it hasn't. We are releasing the new information in order to better equip the public to assist law enforcement. A copy of the statement will be available as you exit the room after the conference."

He looked down at his sheet of paper and resisted the urge to clear his throat again.

"For the past three years, we have been working tirelessly to find a serial killer who is preying on the young women of New Orleans. Unfortunately, he has struck again, and we feel he is not done for this year."

"While we have not identified the man, we have learned a great deal and wish to share some of what we know with the public. We realize the good people of New Orleans have no tolerance for an *animal* such as this." He paused briefly to let the word *animal* sink in. "As a result, I am about to list the basic elements of the crimes and encourage people to study them."

"One, the victims are all African-American females in their early twenties."

He hesitated between each point.

"Two, the victims were all enrolled in a city college or university.

"Three, the killings have all occurred in the first quarter of the year.

"Four, the victims were kept hostage for at least two days before being killed."

He paused a little longer this time, taking a slow breath.

"Fifth and final point…all the victims died from blood loss due to exsanguination through the wrists."

There was a brief gasp from the students at the back. He pushed on.

"The importance of these facts is as follows: As to points one and two, we are asking all female, African-American college students in the Greater New Orleans area to take extra precautions for their safety. While there is no proof that another student of a different race is immune from being taken, we feel it is unlikely. In conjunction with that, point three is meant to suggest that hyper-vigilance is necessary during these early months of the year. Again, that is based on the killer's past behavior."

Vince had never experienced such deafening silence. He paused to look up, and not a single hand was raised. The only noise was him shuffling his notes to the next page.

"As to point four, we are asking the public to take note of any odd behavior or change in routine from those around them. Anything out of the ordinary that might say someone is at a residence where they shouldn't be.

"And finally, point five. When a person dies from a loss of blood, there is a lot to clean up. If someone has found blood—whether recently or in the past three years—that they thought was from an animal, please contact the tip line. Also, if you see someone cleaning carpets repeatedly or throwing away furniture, we would also like to hear from you."

He folded the sheets and put them in his jacket pocket. "Thank you in advance for your help."

When he looked up, literally every hand in the room was raised. He started with the reporter from Tulane.

"Yes, ma'am?"

"Do you have an idea why all the victims are African-American?"

"I do not." He intentionally used the pronoun "I" in his answer. Nikki was to remain anonymous. "I suspect it is either because he is more comfortable moving within those circles, or it fits into his motivation somehow."

Vince moved his gaze to the right side of the room and began working his way across, one hand at a time, pointing. "Yes?"

"Does the blue car belong to Brandi Cole?"

"It does not."

"Whose is it?"

He hesitated. If he said it belonged to the first victim, then they would connect them directly and assume Brandi was dead. That wouldn't help their search.

"I'm afraid I can't reveal that information at this time." Point. "Yes?"

"Have you recovered any DNA?"

"I'm not at liberty to answer that."

He pointed. "Yes?"

"The cause of death—exsanguination—did it result in a total loss of blood volume?"

"Yes."

"So there were no other injuries?"

"Just some bruising."

"Where and from what?"

"I can't go into that."

Again, he pointed. "Yes?"

"Did you find the blood?"

Vince shook his head. "We have never found any of the victims' blood."

Point. "Yes?"

"When and where was Brandi Cole last seen?"

"Late Sunday afternoon at Couturie Forest in City Park."

Rising from her seat without waiting to be called on, the reporter from *The Advocate* cleared her throat. Vince waited as the room—either out of fear or respect—seemed to give the senior reporter the floor. She flipped her black hair over shoulders, turned her blue-green eyes toward him, and smiled. Xavier Warren could be warm and friendly…or as cold as a viper.

Vince steeled himself to find out which had shown up this morning.

"Detective Wills, have you had a profile done by the FBI?"

"Yes. Two years ago."

"Can you share it with us?"

"Not at this time."

She hesitated, then the smile disappeared.

"Isn't it true, Detective Wills, that you believed the killer was done?"

The viper had appeared.

Vince clenched his teeth, and his answer came out as a hiss. He had some snake in him, too.

"In cases such as this, the perpetrator almost never deviates from his M.O., and when a third victim was not found last year, I had *hoped* he had been incarcerated or died. I never considered the case to be solved."

"But you retired."

He bit his tongue. "What is your point?"

"Would you have done so if you thought the killer was still out there?"

Even though he had agreed to return and work the case, Vince had not signed up for this particular kind of abuse. "Miss Warren, do you have a question related to the information provided today?"

She sniffed. "Detective Wills, do you think the killings are tied in some way to Mardi Gras?"

He sighed. "I know that you in the media have dubbed him the Mardi Gras Killer, but as of yet, we have nothing concrete to confirm the theory."

She tucked her pad away, and the room seemed to be holding its collective breath.

"Detective Wills, do you believe the blood is being taken for a ritual, such as the type of ceremonies practiced by those who follow Voodoo teachings?"

He was ready for this one. "That has been suggested before but seems unlikely."

"Why?"

"Because the victims, other than the obvious fact they were killed, were not brutalized. Traditional Voodoo does not treat people viciously, but those that pervert the practice do so with violence, and we see greater trauma to the victims."

It sounded good. Would she buy it?

"I see. Then, Detective Wills, what motive do *you* believe drives the killer."

Vince thought about it. It seemed he was always thinking about it. It was time to go off script. "My personal opinion?"

Xavier Warren nodded and sat down. Vince didn't have to look behind him to know his superiors were boring holes into the back of his head with their gazes. He tipped the mic upward slightly and raised his voice.

"I *think* he believes his ritual, or whatever he calls it, gives him a sense of purpose. I *believe* the blood he takes serves a selfish goal, such as trying to live longer or protect himself from some perceived evil. I *think* he sees himself as justified in doing what he does. I *believe* he doesn't know how sick he is and that he's evil. He needs to be put down like a rabid dog!"

The room fell into another stunned silence. Vince's ears filled with the sound of rushing blood from his surging pulse. From behind, Jacobs stepped forward to the mic.

"Thank you for coming. The handouts will be at the door as you leave. Good day."

Jacobs shut off the mic, glared at Vince, then headed backstage. Nikki waited until Jacobs and Baker had passed then followed them. Beverly Cole and Vince brought up the rear.

Back inside the ready room, Jacobs whispered to the lieutenant then turned to make sure Nikki had escorted Beverly Cole into the hallway before he spun back at Vince.

"Have you lost your mind?"

Vince's head felt as if it might explode. His anger had gotten the better of him, something he'd never experienced before.

"I didn't mean for that to happen."

"I hope not! Perhaps I can tell the mayor you lost your mind."

Baker was mute, and Vince opted for the same course.

Jacobs eyes flared. "You'll be lucky if the mayor doesn't totally disown you and send you back into retirement with a swift kick."

He'd weathered barrages from superiors before, and just then, it was the least of Vince's concerns.

What if he'd gone too far in the killer's eyes? Would he decide to show his displeasure by ramping up the killings? Would more women die because of Vince's fit of anger?

The fear choked him. How would he live with the guilt?

Nikki, who, true to her word, had remained silent during the conference, returned from the hallway.

Jacobs stared at the two of them, rubbing his hands together feverishly. "Let's just hope this works!"

He stormed out of the room.

Nikki let out a low whistle. "Oh, it'll work. He'll react, I'm sure of that, but how?"

Vince let out a long sigh. How, indeed?

Home of Vince and Rose Wills
Memphis Street
Lakeview Neighborhood
North New Orleans
10:15 a.m.

Rose cradled a coffee mug between her hands and watched as Vince left the stage. Probably no one was caught more off guard to see Vince lose his cool than she was. Her husband could control his emotions in the worst of situations, which she'd witnessed many times over the years of their marriage.

At the same time, a moment of reflection told her she shouldn't be surprised. No case had ever weighed on her husband as this one did. She'd watched it steal his sleep, his appetite, and his confidence. Over the past three years, he'd aged ten.

Her phone startled her out of the daydream.

"Hello?"

"Did you know about this?"

Her lips curled into a smile. If she didn't recognize the voice, she would know the passion. Apparently, Domm had seen the press conference. Rose kept her response measured—better to conceal her own concerns.

"Of course."

"Why?"

"Why what?"

Her daughter's exasperation flowed through the receiver. "Why did you let him go back?"

"I didn't *let* him go back. We discussed it."

"Did you tell him you were against it?"

She and Vince had always been open with Domm and Alicia. Family decisions were just that, choices made by the whole family, and they had always encouraged their daughters to think for themselves. Sometimes, Domm took it to the extreme.

"Actually, no. I told him he *should* go back."

Dominique was rarely speechless, but apparently, this statement did the job. The silence lasted so long, Rose looked at her phone to see if the call had been disconnected.

When her daughter spoke again, the wind seemed to have left her sails.

"I don't understand. You and Dad were finally enjoying life beyond his duties. Why let that world back in?"

Rose considered attempting to explain how, like the military, law enforcement, never really lets a former member go, and that the best way to let her husband move forward was to let him go back. Nevertheless, she sensed Domm couldn't really understand and perhaps only a spouse could.

"I love your father, Domm, and he loves me. He would do anything for me, and I for him. You'll just have to trust me when I say it was the right thing to do."

Another long pause. "I love you, Mom."

"I love you, too. Gotta run."

"Bye."

Rose hung up the phone and stared at the TV. A young, female reporter was referring to the case and the connection with area colleges. Rose had fought against it, but now her thoughts went to Alicia. Their daughter fell into the unpleasant category of a prime target, and until the killer was off the streets, she had two people to worry over, not just one.

She shut off the TV and went to refill her coffee mug. She wasn't sure if Vince would be home for dinner—in fact, she doubted it—but she should still take something out of the freezer, just in case.

Saint Vincent De Paul Cemetery #2
Soniat Street
South New Orleans
11:20 p.m.

He turned off Soniat Street onto Loyola Avenue, parked on the grass next to the cemetery, and killed his lights. The burial grounds, surrounded by a low, red-brick wall and accessed through small, steel gates, closed at four in the afternoon, but he always came at night, and no one had ever bothered him.

A cloudless sky, warm breeze, and full moon made for a pleasant evening to visit. He got out of the car and climbed over the wall. The double-crypt bearing his family name lay just a few yards from the road, and the moonlight was more than sufficient for him to make his way over.

The names and life dates of his mother and father, now together and never to be apart again, were engraved on either side of a blank space. This was where he would be laid to rest and where they would reunite as a family forever. In the meantime, he had important work to do.

That work, and the news conference held by the New Orleans PD, had led him to visit this night.

The detective had so much wrong. Whatever profile he was using had completely missed the mark on why the women had to be sacrificed. Nothing personal was gained when the girls died, and the motivation wasn't selfish.

But the errors on the detective's part were actually good news. The bottom line? Don't allow the detective to find him—so many lives depended on it.

He often came to see his parents when decisions had to be made. He craved the closeness to his parents, his father in particular. In darker times, he'd considered trying to contact his father's spirit by delving into the evil of séances, but he'd never believed in such things, and he wasn't going to start now.

He crouched down and laid two magnolia blossoms on the tomb. His thoughts went to the body and what he should do. How could he reveal the victim without jeopardizing everything? A single slip-up during communication could have disastrous consequences for everyone involved—but she deserved to be found. She had earned a proper burial.

Pushing his black, thick-framed glasses back up on his nose, he stood and drew in a long breath.

His father's words came to him.

Do the right thing, especially when no one is looking.

There was only one choice.

Thursday, February 1

Major Crimes Division
715 South Broad Avenue
Mid-City
7:15 a.m.

After the press conference, a small army of uniformed officers had been assigned to the tip line. Calls had come in almost immediately and continued late into the night. When Vince arrived back at the precinct the next morning, the flow of calls had restarted, mostly due to the morning newspapers coming out. He and Nikki had sorted leads until almost eleven the previous night and had been back at it since six-thirty in the morning.

Each tip had to be reviewed, catalogued, and assigned a priority. Any information that appeared especially interesting were assigned a level one tag. Moderate urgency received a level two, and tips that required checking but did not seem significant were labeled a level three. The crackpot leads, when they could be discerned, were level four and would not be followed up on until everything else had been checked out.

Vince tossed another lead on to the level four pile. "Look at that."

Nikki glanced up from her seat at the conference table. "What?"

"The level four pile. It's got a life of its own."

Nikki smiled. "I know. Don't get too close, or it might suck you in."

"I have no doubt. Have you got a *good* lead yet?"

101

She shook her head. "Not a one."

Neither of them had assigned a level 1 rating to a single call, but perhaps more worrisome was the lack of response from their killer. They had hoped he'd take the bait and call in. Not that they would be able to trace the number— obviously, he was too smart for that—but perhaps noise in the background or a careless word would give them a trail to follow.

Vince stood and stretched. His gaze went to the photo of Brandi Cole.

Where was she? Was she still alive? Was the killer with her, or had he dumped her already? Would they soon get a call about a body being found?

He reviewed his long-held image of the killer. Ever since the profile had come back from the FBI, Vince had formed a picture of what he thought his target looked like.

To the profile description—African-American, twenty-five to thirty, clean-cut, athletic, and friendly—Vince's mind added the traits of tall, thin, wears glasses, and has perfect teeth. The resulting image gave him something to focus on when he thought about his killer's next move.

Not that the mental picture helped the case any, but an experienced detective would always try to get inside his adversary's mind—just not for too long. In the cat and mouse game of murderer versus investigator, knowing how your opponent thought was a critical advantage.

More tip sheets landed on the table in front of him. With a groan, he picked up his coffee mug and went after a refill. When he returned, Nikki was on a call. She looked up at him, her wide eyes stopping him in his tracks. She held out a tip sheet, and Vince read over the details. The phone number and address were followed by a note from the officer who took the call.

Thinks she received a note from the killer.

Vince's pulse surged.

Nikki was ending the call. "Yes, ma'am. Thank you. Please don't touch it again until we get there."

She slammed down the phone. "He bit!"

Home of Lucille Howard
College Street
Slidell, Louisiana
9:45 a.m.

Just over twenty-five minutes later, after a pretty trip along Interstate 10 through Bayou Sauvage National Wildlife Refuge and across the eastern mouth of Lake Ponchartrain, Vince and Nikki arrived in Slidell. Used by many as a bedroom community for New Orleans, Slidell offered families a place to live outside the city but still commute to work.

The address on College Street belonged to a small, clapboard home with a tiny front porch and an immaculate front yard. The yellow house was trimmed in white and had an American flag hanging from a post off the porch.

Lucille Howard sat on the porch in a wooden rocker, waiting for them. The dark-skinned woman sported a yellow sundress that matched her home and had her black hair pulled tight behind her head. Vince guessed the thin woman to be in her fifties, but her eyes were tired and looked faded. In contrast, her voice was strong, even forceful.

"You must be the detectives."

Nikki showed her badge. "Yes, ma'am. I'm Detective Santiago—we spoke on the phone."

"Thank you for coming out so quickly."

"Of course. Thank you for calling. This is my partner, Detective Wills."

Vince nodded. "Nice to meet you, ma'am."

"Likewise, Detective. Call me Lucy."

Nikki stepped up onto the porch. "Can I see the letter?"

Lucy gestured toward the small side table next to her rocker. "It's right there. Haven't touched it since I called."

Nikki pulled on gloves. "Did it come in the mail today?"

"Nope. It was pinned under my windshield wiper this morning."

Vince glanced around the front of the house. "Do you have a security camera?"

Lucy shook her head. "Can't afford one."

He made a mental note to canvas the neighborhood for video surveillance. "Why did you call the hotline?"

"Read the note, and you'll see."

Nikki picked up the plain envelope laying across two folded sheets of paper. She looked at it briefly then handed it to Vince. Wearing a pair of evidence-collection gloves, he studied the writing. *Important* was handwritten in a combination of script and block letters.

Vince dropped the envelope into an evidence bag as Nikki handed him one of the sheets of paper. A chill crawled up his spine when he saw it. A map with a bold X alongside a major highway. He recognized the name—Paris Road. It ran north and south through the outfall canal area, a swampy bayou on the east side of New Orleans. He added the sheet of paper to the evidence bag.

Nikki was holding the other sheet out to him. Vince took the note, which was handwritten in cursive on what appeared to be plain white copy paper. The letter was short and to the point.

To whom it may concern,
        The third girl from last year is still out there.
        She deserves to be found and has earned a proper burial.
Mardi Gras

The only other thing on the page ran across the bottom and was printed in bold block lettering.

"GREATER LOVE HATH NO MAN THAN THIS, THAT HE MAY LAY DOWN HIS LIFE FOR HIS FRIENDS." – John 15:13

Vince stared at the quote, a knot forming in his stomach.

What—in the name of all that's holy—did that mean? Were they looking for a religious nut? A zealot? Was he referring to himself, or did it mean he was coming after the detectives searching for him?

When Vince looked up, Nikki and Lucy were both watching him. The world seemed to have paused. A pair of mourning doves cooed from somewhere behind the house and provided the only sound, but otherwise, even the breeze was still. If they were waiting for him to say something, he didn't know what. He was speechless.

Finally, Nikki turned to Lucy. "Do you have any idea why he sent the note to you?"

Lucy stared up at them, and her eyes reddened. "Isn't it obvious?"

Nikki glanced at Vince then back at Lucy. "I'm sorry? Isn't what obvious?"

Lucy eyes welled up, and she extended an unsteady hand toward the note in Vince's possession.

"The girl is my daughter."

Vince's mind spun, and the pounding of his heart thumped in his ears.

Nikki was staring at Lucy as if the woman was speaking Chinese.

"Your daughter? Why would it be your daughter?"

It was Lucy's turn to look surprised. "My daughter has been missing for nearly a year."

Vince's stomach churned. A realization came sweeping over him like a painful tsunami. The previous year—when he thought the pattern had been broken—there had been a third victim all along.

Nikki lowered herself into the rocking chair next to Lucy and studied the woman's face. "I'm sorry, Lucy, but we didn't know your daughter was missing."

Lucy snorted. "Don't surprise me none. The Slidell police have acted like they didn't know either."

"You reported your daughter missing to them a year ago?"

Lucy wiped at the tears on her face. "That's right. They said she had run off, but I know my Desiree, and she wouldn't leave without telling me."

Vince's shock quickly morphed into anger. He yanked out his phone and dialed 9-1-1.

"Saint Tammany Parish 9-1-1. What is your emergency?"

"This is Detective Wills with the New Orleans Police Department. I need you to connect me with the Slidell detective division."

"Uh, well, I can give you the number to the station."

"Never mind that. Just punch me through."

"Very well. Please hold."

A few moments and one click later, a voice came on the phone.

"Major Crimes. Detective Kaminsky."

"Detective, this is Vince Wills from Homicide in New Orleans. Are you familiar with the missing persons case of Desiree Howard?"

"Yes, I am."

"What is the status of that case?"

"The last time I checked—"

"When was that?"

"Probably two months ago."

"Two months ago?" He looked at Lucy.

The older woman rolled her eyes.

Kaminsky's tone turned defensive. "Yeah. I believe it's still listed as a voluntarily missing adult."

Vince was past caring about hurt feelings or police protocol. "Do you know where Mrs. Howard lives?"

"I do."

"Then you might want to get off your butt and come over here. Her missing daughter has most likely always been a murder victim."

Vince hung up.

Lucy was nodding as she wiped away tears. "Now you understand why I said thank you for coming out."

NEW ORLEANS HOMICIDE

Paris Road
Bayou Bienvenue Central Wetland
East of New Orleans
1:15 p.m.

The mark on the map correlated with a small electrical supply warehouse on the east side of Paris Road. With Kaminsky following in a separate car, they had arrived to find the area behind the business was a wetland…bordered on one side by a junkyard and on the other by water.

Vince stood next to Nikki as they stared out toward the swampy mess. "This explains why she was never found."

Nikki groaned. "Yeah, and we're going to need luck to find anything left of her. There are 'gators around here."

Vince snorted. "We live in the bayous—there are 'gators everywhere."

Kaminsky joined them. "Looks formidable."

Vince wiped sweat from his brow. The sun was directly overhead now, and the day was suggesting the warmer weather of spring wasn't far off. He couldn't see a reasonable way to search the area. "Let's go around to the salvage yard and see if the access is better from there."

Along the way, Kaminsky filled them in on the neighborhood canvas. "My officers located one home with a security camera, but unfortunately, it was aimed at an alley behind the house."

Vince nodded. "What about witnesses?"

"No luck on that front, either."

"Can't say I'm surprised."

They turned down Bolivar Lane, which ran east from Paris Road and served more or less as a driveway for the salvage yard. Twenty yards down the lane, they arrived at the office. A man in his late sixties gave them a sideways look. His greasy ball cap was pushed back on his head, and he was eating an apple with hands that were equally greasy. "What can I do for you folks?"

Vince showed his badge. "I'm Detective Wills with the New Orleans PD. My partners and I would like to take a walk through your yard."

"You lookin' for something particular?"

Vince was tempted to blurt out, "Yeah, *a body,*" but thought better of it. "We're searching for someone, and your business backs up to the area we are interested in."

The man, who had not offered to identify himself and whose uniform had no nametag, shrugged. "Help yourself."

"Thank you."

Vince led the way back outside and around the building. The wetlands pushed up against the junk vehicles strewn down Bolivar Lane, threatening to absorb some of them so that they would never be found again. Everywhere they searched for a path or way into the overgrowth, they were met by a sloppy mess.

After a few minutes, Vince threw up his hands. "This isn't going to help. For one thing, we're not dressed for this kind of search."

Nikki wiped at her forehead while Kaminsky, who had been more forceful at trying to penetrate the swamp, picked thorns from his pants.

From somewhere deep in the junkyard, a barking dog triggered a light bulb moment for Vince. "Roberts! Let's get his cadaver dog out here and see if he can penetrate this stuff."

Nikki was all for it. "Great idea."

Vince took out his phone and made the call.

Lower Ninth Ward
New Orleans
2:45 p.m.

Quite sure the note had been found by now, he was tempted to take a drive along Paris Road and look for activity, but that would be foolish, not to mention risky. He grabbed a water bottle from the fridge and went into the bedroom. No longer shrinking away every time he entered, she instead met him with a blank stare. He tossed the bottle onto the bed.

She ignored it. "I told you I'm hungry."

He nodded. "And I told you no food. Water is all you get now."

"Why?"

"Because your blood must be cleansed of impurities."

"So you said. What I mean is, why are you doing this to me?"

"It's not personal. You happened to be chosen."

"For what?"

"We've discussed that, too—a sacrifice."

Her eyes welled up as her anger surged. "For what, you sicko?"

He regarded her coolly, the show of defiance of little consequence to him. "You wouldn't understand if I told you, so why bother? Just accept that your life is going to save hundreds, maybe thousands of others."

Her body vibrated as she seethed. "You have no right!"

"I not only have the right but the duty."

She grabbed the plastic bottle and hurled it at him.

He dodged it easily. "You'll want that."

He retrieved it and tossed it back on the bed then left before she could throw it again.

It had seemed fortuitous at the time when he'd gotten two women in one swoop, but now, he questioned the wisdom of taking both. Having the girl under his roof left him vulnerable to outside snooping and accidental discovery. In the future, he would keep it to one subject at a time.

Paris Road
Bayou Bienvenue Central Wetland
East of New Orleans
4:10 p.m.

Lieutenant Greg Roberts rolled up in his red Chevy Tahoe with the New Orleans Fire Department insignia emblazoned on the side and paused at the edge of the yellow crime scene tape. The officer on duty lifted the tape and allowed him to steer his vehicle down Bolivar Lane.

Pacing back and forth in the rear seat, the lieutenant's large companion stared eagerly at the group of detectives standing next to the junkyard office. Roberts glanced in the rearview and smiled.

"Easy, Char."

The dog settled down immediately, sitting erect, her eyes laser focused ahead.

Roberts parked and got out. A twenty-three-year veteran of the New Orleans Fire and Rescue, he remained fit and trim, never letting age or rank be an excuse for an expanding mid-section. He'd been a canine officer for five years, and his four-legged partner had no patience for a handler who wasn't able to keep up. The lanky, black and tan Belgian Malinois was agile and swift, so for their searches to be successful, Roberts had to match her stamina and intensity.

The partnership with Char—short for Charlemagne— was both rewarding and stomach churning. Their teamwork often ended with satisfaction when Char found her target but was quickly followed by a sadness that comes with locating somebody's loved one. The physical and emotional toll of the assignments required a special breed—of dog and person.

Roberts spotted his old friend, Vince Wills, striding toward him. "Greg! Thanks for coming."

"Vince? They told me you called, but I figured they were mistaken. I thought you were off fishing somewhere."

"I was, at least, figuratively. A call from Ted Baker changed that."

"What have you got for Char and me?"

"This." The detective handed him a photocopy of a map. "We received it today and believe it's the location of a missing woman. Unfortunately, she's been gone for nearly a year, and combined with the nearly impenetrable brush, we haven't had any luck finding her."

Greg studied the map, then looked toward the swampy area. "So, what you're saying is, I'm gonna wish you stayed retired."

Vince laughed. "Pretty much."

Greg gave the map back to Vince and headed around the back of the junkyard office. He quickly ruled out entering through that way if he could avoid it. With Vince trailing him, he went back out onto Bolivar Lane and around to the electrical supply business.

Behind the metal structure, the swamp pushed up to within feet of the gravel. While almost as daunting, it appeared the best route for him and Char. "We'll start here."

Vince shrugged. "You're in charge."

Greg returned to his vehicle. Char's brown eyes were riveted to him, and the closer he got, the faster her tail pitched back and forth. He grabbed a leash, opened the back door, and clipped the lead to Char's orange search vest. She dropped down out of the vehicle, ready to work.

After walking her over to the area he'd chosen, he had her sit next to him. She stayed perfectly still, looking up at him. He re-tied his waterproof boots, repositioned the chaps he wore over his jeans, and zipped his search coat tight. After pulling down a hat to protect his head, he looked at Char. Only the whiskers on her face twitched—nothing else moved. He unclipped the leash, put a hand by her nose, swung it in the direction of the brush, and barked a single word.

"Hunt!"

Within moments, she was leading him through paths big enough for her but not him, meaning he spent much of the time trying to stay low to the ground. Char surged in one direction, dismissed it, and then rotated back another way. Occasionally, she'd pause to scent the air then put her nose back down and push forward.

This went on for nearly ten minutes, until she suddenly froze. Two sharp barks told him she had scented something.

He caught up with her and kneeled beside her, stroking her head.

"Good girl, Char. Stay."

A small clearing had held the brush at bay. Greg guessed they were no more than thirty yards from the back of the electrical supply shop. He crept forward, scanning the damp ground. A whitish-colored object, which he quickly recognized as a femur, protruded from the weeds.

He stepped back and keyed his radio. "Wills?"

"Go ahead."

"I've got something."

Home of Lucille Howard
College Street
Slidell, Louisiana
6:45 p.m.

Two hours later, the site had been secured. Excavation had begun and would go on well into the night and most of the next day. After that, they would hope for a positive identification. It wouldn't be accomplished with fingerprints or photographs—decomposition had removed those options—but hopefully, they'd ID the body using dental records or DNA.

Vince had dropped Nikki at the precinct so she could go over the file provided by Kaminsky. If their assumption was correct and they'd found Desiree Howard, they'd need to know everything they could about their latest victim.

Meanwhile, he'd taken it upon himself to visit Lucille Howard. She deserved to be kept informed, regardless of how little they knew for sure. Kaminsky had offered to come along, but considering the animosity Lucille held for the Slidell police, Vince chose to tell her alone.

She was on the porch, rocking in the same chair, almost as if she hadn't moved since he left her there some eight hours before. She managed a weak smile as he came up the steps.

"Good evening, Detective. I gather you have news."

He gestured toward the other rocker. "May I?"

"By all means. Would you like something to drink?"

He did, but wanted to get the task over with, so he deferred. "No, thank you. You're correct, I do have news."

She stopped rocking. "Did you find my Desiree?"

He nodded. "We believe so, at least, we found remains where the map indicated."

She resumed rocking, her gaze moving to the darkening sky. "It's her. I know it."

"I'm sorry."

She turned toward him, her eyes sad but dry. "Have you ever had a loved one go missing, Detective?"

"No, ma'am."

"I'm glad. You don't want to be a member of that club, I assure you. It's a terrible place to be. Searching while you have hope, then hoping but running out of places to search. Eventually, just praying for the not-knowing to end."

"I can't imagine."

"And there's only one way out of that club. You only get out when your loved one is found—be it dead or alive."

"I'm sorry it wasn't the better of the two."

"Thank you, and though you might not understand it, thank you for the news."

He didn't know what to say.

Apparently sensing his struggle, she stopped rocking. "Detective, as you are aware more than most, death is a part of living. Some are granted long life, and others have it cut short, but for all, death is inevitable. I can bury my daughter now, and I can mourn her death. That, at least, is a natural part of life." She stood. "Not knowing if my daughter was alive or dead, that was unnatural. It is like dying without death and living without life."

She opened the screen door. "I imagine you will want my daughter's dental records. I read that someone who's missing a loved one should have a set for identification."

"That would be very helpful…" He choked on the words.

Concern on her face, she reached out and touched his hand. "Are you sure you don't want something to drink?"

He looked at her glass on the little table between them. "What are you drinking?"

"Sweet tea with lemon."

"That would be nice."

She smiled, and to Vince, the smile was different somehow. Perhaps the smile of someone at peace.

She patted his hand. "I'll be right back."

<u>Friday, February 2</u>

Major Crimes Division
715 South Broad Avenue
Mid-City
7:00 a.m.

On the way in to the precinct, Vince had stopped and given Chris Nagle the dental records Lucille Howard had provided. Nagle hoped to have a forensic odontologist look at them before lunch.

Since arriving back at the office, Vince had been sitting in the conference room with Nikki as she brought him up-to-speed on their assumed victim, Desiree Howard.

"African-American, twenty-seven years old, reported missing January 31 of last year. Phone conversation with her mother on the day before was last known contact. Lucille stated her daughter was headed into New Orleans to attend a Mardi Gras parade with some friends but never showed."

"That fits so far. What else?"

"She was in her final semester at Delta College in Slidell. She was getting her LPN certification."

"She's the first who was not from a four-year college and the first who wasn't going to school in New Orleans. That might help explain why she didn't pop up on the radar for our case."

Nikki sighed. "Yeah, that and incompetent detective work."

Though he agreed, he held his tongue. There was no point in wasting energy on things they couldn't do anything about. He picked up his photocopy of the map.

The corners had been trimmed to remove all identifying marks such as date, time, and website. Still, there had to be a way to get something from it.

"Who's working with the map in forensics?"

Nikki glanced at a note. "Piper McCarty."

"Doesn't ring a bell for me. You?"

She shook her head. "Never met her."

Vince stood. "Then let's do just that. You drive."

Crime Lab and Evidence Division
University of New Orleans Research
& Technology Park
Gentilly District
North New Orleans
8:45 a.m.

Pressed up against the south shore of Lake Ponchartrain sat the University of New Orleans technology park. The Crime Scene Unit, Criminalistics Unit, and the Forensic Support Unit were all housed within this complex.

For Vince and his detective colleagues, this was *the* key support group. Answers to questions— some that no one had even thought to ask just a decade before—came out of this place on a daily basis. As a man with limited scientific knowledge, Vince considered what these experts did to be nothing short of magic.

The weather had taken a turn toward the chillier side, with a cold front making it all the way to the gulf the night before. The cooler air was accompanied by a gusty wind, and small whitecaps could be seen far out in the lake.

On the second floor, Vince and Nikki found a small office with a door plaque that read: *Computer Forensics—Piper McCarty*. Vince tapped on the doorframe.

"Excuse me?"

A young lady dressed in a long white lab coat—Vince guessed her to be in her late twenties or early thirties—looked toward the door.

"Yes?"

"Miss McCarty?"

"That's right. Can I help you?"

"My name is Detective Wills. This is my partner, Detective Santiago."

She smiled brightly and pushed a lock of dirty-blonde hair from in front of her glasses. "Oh, hi. You're the detectives who sent the map, right?"

"Yes. May we come in?"

"Of course. I was just working on it."

Vince moved over to where he could look over the technician's shoulder. "Any luck?"

"Nothing definitive yet."

Nikki leaned against the doorframe. "What kind of information do you think you might get?"

Piper McCarty rotated her chair back to the tall lab table covered with computer equipment. Three monitors were accompanied by three keyboards, a printer, and a scanner. She gestured at the screen on the left, which showed a magnified version of the map.

"As you know, the map had been trimmed of its identifying characteristics, but that doesn't mean we can't determine which site produced it."

"Really? How?"

"Well, to start with, there are the big three services. The vast majority of online maps are obtained from Google Maps, Microsoft's Bing Maps, and MapQuest. In addition to those, there are roughly a dozen smaller sites. Each of those sites has distinct variations in how the maps are presented."

Vince stared at the map on the screen. It looked like every other map to him. "What kind of variations?"

"Things like alignment, orientation, and information provided, such as landmarks."

"What can you get from that?"

Piper was warming to the task and obviously enjoyed her work. "Usually, I can get an ISP."

Vince looked at Nikki with a raised eyebrow.

Nikki grinned. "Internet service provider."

Vince nodded. That, he had heard of. "Like AT&T?"

Piper's head bobbed enthusiastically. "Exactly."

"Does the ISP give you a name?"

"No, it's a set of numbers, but we can find out who uses the ISP from the provider."

Nikki came over to look at the screens and pointed at the center one.

"What are you searching here?"

Piper punched the corresponding keyboard, and a map flashed onto the screen. "This is the map for Paris Road that Bing provided. As you can see, if I magnify it to the same size as the one you submitted, there are several differences."

Vince spotted one immediately. "It doesn't show the electric supply house."

Piper grinned. "Right. So I can eliminate this map as being the source."

"And eliminate Bing?"

"No, not yet. For example, I need to do the same search with nearby businesses noted."

Vince's hopes were growing quickly. "When do you think you'll get a result?"

The tech shrugged. "Hard to say. If the perp used a small company, it could take days. If he used a big service, I might have something for you later today."

"And after that—the name?"

"That's where it gets sticky. The map services are pretty quick about responding to subpoenas, but the ISPs are notoriously slow. It's a crap-shoot on how fast."

Vince turned to Nikki. "I guess we're just holding the lady up, then."

She nodded and smiled at Piper. "Thanks for your help. Call us when you get something?"

"You'll be the first."

Nikki led the way out. Back to the car, Vince's phone rang.

"Detective Wills."

"Vince, it's Chris Nagle."

"Hey. You have news?"

"I've got the preliminary report done. You want the basics?"

Vince checked the time. "Actually, we're not far from you. We'll come by."

"Perfect. See you soon."

Vince hung. "Next stop, coroner's office."

NEW ORLEANS HOMICIDE

Office of Orleans Parish Coroner
Earhart Boulevard
Central New Orleans
10:30 a.m.

Vince and Nikki found Chris Nagle in his office.
Vince tapped on the door. "Hey, Chris."
"Hi, Vince. Hi, Nikki. Come in."
As was his custom, Vince took a seat. "Is it her?"
Chris nodded. "Dental records matched."
Vince's thoughts went briefly to Lucille Howard.
Nikki, standing in the doorway, took out her notepad.
"Cause of death?"
Chris shrugged. "Undetermined. No blunt force marks
or cuts were located on what skeletal remains we had, except
for what I determine were animal bites, and there was
virtually no flesh remaining. If she was bled out like the
others, I can't prove it."
Vince had expected as much. "Manner of death is
homicide, I assume?"
"Technically, no. Because I don't have a definitive cause,
the death will be listed as undetermined, at least for now."
"What about TOD?"
"Again, that's speculative, but close to her disappearance
is a reasonable assumption. I did recover some hair, and we're
doing drug testing on it, but I don't have the results yet."
Vince sighed. "Anything else?"
Chris shook his head.
Vince stood. "Okay. I guess I have a call to make.
Thanks, Doc."

Vince followed Nikki out into the hallway. "Since you're driving, I think I'll wait until we're in the car to call Lucille Howard."

"You've been doing the tough work, lately. You want me to handle this call?"

He forced a weak smile. "No, but thanks anyway. Besides, she likes me."

Nikki chuckled. "All the ladies like you, Vince."

"Don't tell, Rose."

****

Vince had phoned Lucille on the way back to the precinct. The call went to voicemail, so he'd left a message, but she hadn't gotten back to him yet.

Back at the station, he found a forensic report folder waiting for him on the conference table. He slid into his chair and opened it—it was the results of the testing on the notes. Scanning to the bottom, he found the summary.

"Specimen papers were processed for DNA and prints. Known subject Lucille Howard was identified on envelope, note, and map. No others were found."

"Can't say I'm surprised."

"Surprised about what?"

He looked up to see Nikki watching him. She'd gotten herself a cup of coffee and was leaning against the doorframe of the conference room. He closed the folder. "No prints or DNA were found on the sheets of paper we submitted."

"You're right, that's not a surprise."

Vince sucked in a long breath. "I guess it would be unrealistic to expect our guy to get stupid and careless now."

Lieutenant Baker appeared behind Nikki. "How about an update."

"Yes, sir."

Nikki went around the table and sat down. Baker came in and closed the door. Vince spent the next twenty minutes going over what they had learned in the forty-eight hours since the press conference.

Baker's disappointment was painted across his face "Nothing solid from the autopsy?"

Vince shook his head. "Afraid not. I hate to pin our hopes on the computer stuff, but it's the best thing we have right now. What about the tip line? Anything new?"

Baker shook his head. "I've got an army in blue following up on calls, but most seem to be a waste of time."

Vince's phone rang. "Detective Wills."

"Detective, this is Lucille Howard."

"Hi. Can you hang on a second?"

"Sure."

Vince stood and went outside the room. "Thank you for calling me back."

"You mentioned you had news."

"Yes...the coroner has positively identified the remains we found—it's Desiree."

"As you know, I felt all along it was her. Thank you for calling me."

He detected no change in her demeanor. "Of course. Is there anything else I can do for you?"

"Do you know when the coroner will release my daughter?"

"I don't, but he will call you as soon as he can."

"Very well. Thank you again for all you've done."

The line went dead, and Vince hung up.

When he returned to the conference room, Nikki was alone. "Mrs. Howard?"

He nodded.

"How is she?"

"Okay, I guess." He sighed, and a heavy weariness swept over him. "You know what? I think I'm gonna go home."

Nikki nodded approvingly. "I think that's an excellent idea."

"Let me know if you hear from Piper McCarty."

"I will."

Home of Vincent and Rose Wills
Memphis Street
Lakeview Neighborhood
North New Orleans
3:25 p.m.

The morning chill had given way to the warmth of the Louisiana sun in the afternoon, and the pleasant temperature beckoned Vince out to his back deck. Rose made them each an iced tea and joined him. She handed him the glass and lowered herself onto the swing beside him. Together, they rocked peacefully.

Vince tried to focus on the breeze and the sound it made going through the trees. A long time ago, he'd found the sounds of nature could bring him calm during the storm of his life as a detective. He'd watched more than one investigator get taken down by the sadness and depression that seemed built into the job.

For him, the contrast between the unnatural world, where he spent his workdays, and the ordered existence of the natural galaxy around him, served to bring some balance to a life that could quickly spin wildly out of control.

The light began to dim around them, and their glasses were empty, but Rose had still not broken the silence. In fact, she had set her glass on a side table and taken his hand, holding it on her lap while they rocked.

In the back of his mind, a clock ticked. It had developed while working the case, an almost instinctual tracking of time. From the first murder of each year, he'd heard that same clock counting down to another girl's death, then after that, restarting toward the next murder.

When the third woman was found, the clock reset to a longer countdown—headed toward the start of the following year. But last year, they hadn't found the third victim, and the clock had stopped. Now, it ticked louder than ever.

He squeezed Rose's hand. "Time's running out."

She wrapped his hand between both of hers. "Don't give up. You'll figure it out."

He smiled down at her. She had always believed in him. When others told him to let something go, she pushed him on, usually to success. And when he did fall short, she picked him up, dusted him off, and sent him back at it. He'd given up trying to figure out why and had just accepted how lucky he was to have her.

His stomach grumbled. "Did you have something planned for dinner, Rose?"

"Yes, but that was before you came home early."

"You want to go out to eat?"

"Are you asking me out on a date, Mr. Wills?"

"Indeed, I am. Do you have time in your busy schedule?"

"For you, sir, I always have time."

He lifted her hand to his lips and kissed it. "I'll clean up, and we'll go."

"Perfect."

NEW ORLEANS HOMICIDE

<u>Saturday, February 3</u>

Major Crimes Division
715 South Broad Avenue
Mid-City
7:45 a.m.

Nikki arrived at the precinct and immediately went to the conference room. Her hopes of finding a note from Piper McCarty were quickly dashed. That left her with nothing to do, so she retrieved the log of phone tips from the previous night. They had slowed to a trickle, and still, nobody had provided them with a solid lead.

Then again, why should the public have better luck than the police had when it came to tracking this guy down? Still, it was disappointing.

"Good morning."

She looked up to find Vince coming through the door.

"Morning to you. How was your evening?"

"Nice. I took Rose to one of her favorite places for dinner."

"And that is?"

"Antoine's"

Nikki let out a low whistle. "Oh, my. That was nice of you. That place is exquisite."

His grin had a sheepish air to it. "She deserved it."

"I have no issue with that. After all, she's put up with you for how many years?"

He scowled at her. "Now, just you never mind."

"What did you have?"

"Crab Amandine and she had Grilled Pompano."

"Don't you mean Pompano Grillé?"

He laughed. "If I spoke Creole—yes."

Her face twisted into a frown. "I had canned chili for dinner."

"Glad I didn't bring her to your place."

He sat down just as Nikki's phone rang.

"Detective Santiago."

"Yes, this is Piper McCarty."

Nikki flipped her gaze up to Vince and raised an eyebrow. "Yes, Piper. How is the search going?"

"I've made a significant connection."

"Really? Like what?"

"Well—"

"Hold on while I put you on speaker. Detective Wills is here." Nikki pushed the button and laid the phone on the table. "Go ahead."

"Good morning, Detective Wills."

"Morning."

"As I was saying to your partner, I've made a significant connection between the map and the site where it came from."

"Excellent. We're listening."

"The map provided by your suspect was printed off from Yahoo Maps. It's not one of the larger companies, but I'm sure you recognize the name."

Nikki was making notes. "That's excellent. What's the next step?"

"I'm preparing a search warrant for the ISP address."

"How do they narrow it down?"

"That's where I need your help. I can tell them the area—say, southern Louisiana—and a target area, but I need a time window. What are your thoughts on that?"

Nikki looked up at her partner. "What do you think, Vince?"

Vince had closed his eyes and was leaning back in his chair. "Well, it's almost surely tied to the press conference, wouldn't you think?"

"Probably. Xavier Warren brought up the fact that we hadn't found the third victim from last year. The map showed up within twenty-four hours."

Vince rocked forward. "I agree. Miss McCarty, use the past seventy-two hours as your window."

"Very well. I'll send the warrant shortly."

"How long before you get an answer?"

"I can't say for sure, but they won't even receive it until Monday morning. With luck, before the end of the day."

"Excellent. Thank you so much."

"You're very welcome."

Nikki reached for her phone. "Bye." She hung up. "This could be it! The press conference may have done the trick."

"Let's hope you're right."

Lower Ninth Ward
New Orleans
9:00 a.m.

The coppery smell of blood filled the inside of the tiny house. While not an odor he enjoyed, he could tolerate it, especially considering the importance of the task that produced it. Still, he'd be glad when the purification rites were finished for the year.

The effort it took each January to prepare and then carry out the sanctification was becoming more taxing with every passing Mardi Gras season. So far, he'd succeeded in not getting caught, but another group of thoughts had begun to trouble him—the *what ifs.*

What if he was caught? What if he died? What if someone else didn't step up to take his place? What if the sanctifications stopped?

He glanced at the photo from the day he and his father were rescued. The memory of the fear washed over him as if it was yesterday, but a new worry made it worse—the realization that it might all happen again.

M & J Soul Food
Lake Forest Boulevard
East New Orleans
11:30 a.m.

Vince played with the food on his plate, pushing the remainder of his fried okra around with a fork. He'd accepted the invitation from Nikki to have lunch at her expense, mostly to get away from the precinct. She had finished her shrimp basket and was watching him, but he pretended not to notice.

The leads from the tip line had dried up, and what they did have was of no use. The only thing they had going for them was the forensic search being done by Piper McCarty, and since she didn't need help, they were languishing in a kind of holding pattern.

The time remaining on his mental countdown clock was getting ever shorter, and waiting for their next lead meant it may come as another dead body.

Nikki pushed her basket away from her. "I hate having nothing to do but re-read reports I've read a hundred times."

He sighed. "I know how you feel, but what's worse is not having any control over your best lead."

"Piper is on it. I'm sure it will come back soon."

"I hope so."

"I had high hopes for the press conference, and it did draw him out, but not how we thought."

He dropped his fork onto the plate and leaned back. "That's for sure. There was no sense of anger in his note, just news of another body. Not what I was expecting."

She nodded. "Me, neither. Speaking of the unexpected—what about the scripture?"

He crossed his arms and stared at her. "I've run that through my mind over and over again. I can't figure out who he's talking about."

"I tend to believe he's referencing the victims."

"Maybe, but what about himself? Is he suggesting he might kill himself at some time?"

Nikki shook her head. "I don't think so. Doesn't fit with his pattern unless that's his final solution when he's about to be caught."

Vince agreed but was still weighing all possibilities. "Have you considered he might be talking about one of us?"

Her brow furrowed. "Us?"

"Yeah, like we might need to lay down our life for him to remain free."

She ran a hand through her hair. "I hadn't considered it, but it strikes me as unlikely."

He shrugged. "You're probably right."

"What was that?"

"I said, you're probably..."

She was grinning at him.

He laughed. "Okay, very funny. In fact, it's so funny, I'm gonna have a piece of pie at your expense."

"Fine with me. Order two pieces while you're at it. I'm going to the ladies room."

He watched her slip out of her chair and cross the dining room. The future of New Orleans homicide investigations was in good hands with Nikki Santiago. Truth be told, she probably would have been fine without him coming back, but that horse was out of the barn now.

He flagged down the waitress.

17th *Street Canal*
Lakewood District
North-Central New Orleans
11:45 p.m.

He took Interstate 10, known locally as the Ponchartrain Expressway, west through the 7th Ward and Mid-City until it merged with West End Boulevard. A left on Veteran's Boulevard and another left on Fleur-De-Lis Drive brought him to Frontage Road. With each turn, fewer and fewer cars were around, and as he turned west on Frontage, he found himself alone.

Running along a high wall that supported Interstate 610, Frontage Road eventually turned under the freeway. At that spot, he pulled off and killed his lights. With his window open, the cars passing overhead were a steady drone, but no sound came from directly around him.

After fifteen minutes, he climbed out of his van and grabbed the bag containing his cargo. Walking swiftly north, he came to a rise that led up to a concrete wall bordering the Seventeenth Street Canal. The most important canal in the city, its failure during Katrina had cost hundreds of lives. It would not happen again.

He easily scaled the wall, dropped on the canal side of the levee. He stood in silence, letting the memories of Katrina, the fear, and his grandfather wash over him. These moments reminded him why it was all worth doing.

Then he finished his task, and a few minutes later, he was back in his van.

Two down—one to go—the Industrial Canal.

NEW ORLEANS HOMICIDE

Sunday, February 4

Lakewood Country Club
General Degaulle Drive
Southeast New Orleans
6:45 a.m.

Rory Horner turned his pick-up into the empty lot, circled around to the gravel service road, and headed toward the machine shed. His job as Head Groundskeeper meant he was usually one of the first to arrive, but Sundays were a rarity for him. His assistant had asked for the day off for his daughter's birthday party and he'd been happy to oblige the man.

The service road traveled through some trees for about a quarter mile, but he was less than a hundred yards along when something in the roadway stopped him. It had been a long time since he'd seen a deer around, but it was too big to be a skunk or possum—a 'gator maybe?

He put his truck in park and climbed out, approaching cautiously. The cool morning air carried a faint odor he was unfamiliar with. His eyes weren't as good as they used to be, but he quickly determined it wasn't a 'gator. No, it had arms and legs—like a person.

He stopped suddenly and squinted for signs of life. The woman looked asleep, lying on her back with her arms crossed over her chest. Then he saw her eyes. Open, fixed, blank—she was dead.

He back-pedaled rapidly to his truck and called 9-1-1.

"Orleans Parish 9-1-1. Where is your emergency?"

"Lakewood Country Club on Degaulle."

"And what is the problem?"

"There's a dead girl on our service road."

Harbor Community Church
Canal Boulevard
North New Orleans
9:45 a.m.

Vince sat listening to the pastor's sermon and did his best to concentrate, but he was having a hard time. Truth was, if Rose asked him what it was about, he'd be stuck for a good answer. Fortunately, she never checked up on him when he was working a case—she knew he'd have a split attention span—and she'd actually been surprised when he said he was going to church that morning.

Domm and Grace were with them, which was especially nice, even though Domm had taken the opportunity to voice her displeasure at him working again.

"You have to quit sometime, Dad."

"I know that. These are special circumstances."

"So Mom told me. Still, you have to let someone else take over."

"I will, I promise. This is the last case."

She'd stared at him with a skeptical glare then smiled and kissed his cheek. That was that. Alicia would call her mother to ask why he'd gone back to work, but he didn't expect his oldest daughter to voice an opinion either way. She trusted her mother's judgment in these manners.

A vibration from inside his pocket startled him. He reached for his phone and pulled it just far enough from his jacket pocket to see the screen. The name created a sick feeling in the pit of stomach—Ted Baker. He touched Rose on the knee, and she nodded without looking at him. It was their signal after a work related phone call.

He slid out of the pew and went through the double doors leading out from the sanctuary. Using a side exit, he stepped out into the morning sun and called the lieutenant back.

"Lieutenant Baker."

"Hey, Ted. It's me."

"Morning, Vince. I'm afraid I have some bad news."

"Brandi Cole?"

"I believe so. Nikki is on her way out to the scene now."

"Where is it?"

"Lakeview Country Club."

His insides churned as he pictured what she would find. "I'll call Nikki and get an update."

"Let me know."

"Yes, sir."

He hung up and dialed Nikki.

"Been expecting your call."

"I just heard from the lieutenant."

A car door slammed in the background. "I got here two minutes ago."

"Is it her?"

"I don't know. Hold on."

Vince listened as Nikki identified herself.

"She's just down the road," a man responded. "We taped off both ends of this service road and have another officer posted at the other end."

"Thank you."
The sound of shoes dragging on gravel filled the phone for a moment. "Vince?"
"Yeah."
"I'm walking up on the scene now. I can already tell she's positioned like the others."
His heart sank. Any hope it wasn't Brandi left him.
"It's her, Vince."
"Okay. Be out there soon."
He hung up and sent a text to Rose.
Got a scene. Ride with Domm. Call later. Love you.
He closed his phone and climbed into his car.

Lakewood Country Club
General Degaulle Drive
Southeast New Orleans
11:00 a.m.

The coroner's van was still not on site when Vince arrived. Most of the golf club parking lot was cordoned off, and a sign had been posted at the entrance.

Due to unforeseen circumstances, the course will not be open today.
Normal hours will resume on Monday morning.

It was a pleasant euphemism for a dead body—unforeseen circumstances. Vince had heard worse. He squeezed past the group of reporters gathered near the yellow crime tape, flashed his badge, and ducked inside the perimeter without responding to any questions.

He followed the gravel road for about fifty yards before he came around a bend and found the organized chaos of a crime scene. Officers were searching the brush and trees around the perimeter, photos were still being taken, and two techs were examining impressions on the road. Vince reached them first.

"Tire prints?"

One of the officers looked up. "We're hoping to cast them, but this dust is extremely fine. Not sure if it will work."

"Make sure you photograph them completely, first."

"Yes, sir."

Vince moved on a little farther and found Nikki leaning over the body.

"Hey."

She looked back at him, squinting into the sun behind him. "Vince?"

"In person."

She stood. "Everything matches. No blood on site, pale color, X-marks at the wrists."

Vince walked around the body, looking for anything he could find that was outside the M.O. and might tip them off. He found nothing.

He waved an arm at the area search. "Find anything?"

"Not so far."

"Coroner on the way?"

"Yes."

He glanced toward the machine shed at the end of the road. "Who found the body?"

"Groundskeeper. I interviewed him and let him go. He needed to advise the course managers."

"What did he say?"

"He left around dark last night and returned at 6:45 this morning. This road is open to the parking lot at all times, so someone used it during the night."

"Fits with our killer. A country club…he's choosing classier dump spots for his victims."

She groaned. "Ain't nothin' classy about this guy."

"You got that right."

There was very little that could be learned at the site, and one task needed to be done before the press got wind of their victim's identity. They had to see Beverly Cole.

Nikki was watching him and was ahead of him. "She's still at the Days Inn."

He nodded. "Let's go."

Room 159
Days Inn Motel
New Orleans East
12:45 p.m.

Beverly Cole had spent the past week staying at the small motel, mostly waiting by the phone. She would go out for food, then upon returning, immediately check the blinking light on the room phone to see if she had a message. Her cell phone was with her all the time, but it hadn't brought news, either.

Because her daughter was last seen at City Park, she'd spent what energy she did have posting missing flyers featuring a picture of Brandi, the blue VW, and a description.

Beverly had put the tip line number across the bottom, but so far, nothing had come of the posters. She hadn't expected them to do much, especially since the information was all over the local TV stations anyway, but she had to do *something*.

Detective Santiago had checked in by phone every couple of days but never with any news. Beverly suspected only the best or worst news would be shared with her, anyway, in order to protect the investigation.

Sitting on the end of the bed, she stared at the stack of missing flyers on the dresser. She had roughly half what she'd printed remaining. Did she have the energy to go back out again? She wasn't sure. Besides, posting the flyers reminded her of all the TV crime shows she'd watched about missing persons. The family always made posters, but their loved one would turn up dead anyway. As if the posters themselves were bad luck…

"Stop it, Beverly!"

Scolding herself out loud had become a regular occurrence over the course of the last week. Whenever she let negativity take hold, she would talk to herself, reminding herself that she was Brandi's best hope.

She stood and looked into the dresser mirror. She barely recognized the image in front of her. She was down at least ten pounds, and her hair spent day and night in a ponytail. She hadn't opened her make-up bag since the press conference.

Three quick raps on the door startled her, and her heart jumped into her throat as she stared at it.

"Who is it?"

"Detectives Santiago and Wills."

Oh, no. They had always called before. Did them showing up at her door mean the worst had happened?

Her feet remained fixed in place, and her legs refused to move. The room spun, and she had to use the dresser to steady herself.

"Come in."

The door opened slowly, and Santiago's head poked inside. "Mrs. Cole?"

"Yes?"

"May we come in?"

"Yes."

She still hadn't moved, and the spinning in her head had picked up speed. The detective rushed toward her, and Beverly found herself in the woman's arms, being dragged to the bed.

"Mrs. Cole? Mrs. Cole, can you hear me?"

Everything was fuzzy. "Yes."

Detective Wills appeared behind Santiago, a glass of something in his hand. He put it to her lips, and she took a sip. Water. She sipped some more, and her mind began to clear. Eventually, the furniture in the room became stationary, and she was able to sit up.

She finished the last of the water. "You have news?"

Wills put the glass on the side table. "It's Brandi."

"Is she okay?"

"I'm sorry—no."

Everything went black.

Home of Vincent and Rose Wills
Memphis Street
Lakeview Neighborhood
North New Orleans
4:25 p.m.

An ambulance came and transported Beverly Cole to the hospital. Vince and Nikki had followed her and made sure she was okay before heading back to the precinct. Neither he nor Nikki spoke on the way from the hospital to the station, and he'd only nodded when she got out. She drove off without a word.

Some four hours after arriving at the motel, Vince finally came through his own front door. Domm and Grace were gone, and Rose was sitting in the living room waiting for him. When she saw him, she got up and went to the kitchen. She returned with a glass of wine for him and a refill of hers.

They sat together on the couch. Her free hand held his, and the room remained quiet for a long time. Eventually, he couldn't contain it any longer, and tears spilled down his face.

She squeezed his hand. "What happened?"

"We found the second victim."

"I'm sorry."

He pawed at his cheeks. "I knew this would happen."

"What would happen?"

"That the girls would die anyway, and I couldn't stop it."

"You're not done."

He looked at her. "I think I am."

She looked into his eyes, and he could tell she was measuring him. He'd seen it before. She was determining

145

what the best course was to take, the best way to convey her belief in him, to demonstrate her faith in his ability to see it through.

Over their years together, she had chided, cajoled, sweet-talked, and even yelled at him in order to get him to do the right thing, no matter how difficult. And it hadn't always been about work. Sometimes, he needed to apologize to his daughters, or be honest with her about his feelings. Regardless, she was always correct and usually successful.

"Don't tell me you're going to give up and hand the case to Nikki."

He nodded. "I think it's for the best."

"Oh, really? The best for who? Nikki? The next girl to die? You, me?"

He flinched. "I just…"

She had set her glass down and was staring at him with fire in her eyes. "You stepped back into the situation because you believed you were the best man for the job, and I urged you to do it because I felt the same way. What about that belief has changed?"

He met her stare. "I'm not sure anymore."

"Well, you better *get* sure, because lives depend on it. The only thing that has changed is that you've suffered a setback, and we both know that comes with the territory."

She crossed her arms and watched him, waiting.

She was right, of course. If he did quit, he could never live with himself. And worst of all, he would have let her down.

He wiped his cheeks dry and let his lips curl up at the corners. "You're cute when you're mad."

She waved her finger back and forth at him. "Don't you try that nonsense with me, Vincent Stanley Wills, unless you really want to see me mad."

He shook his head. "Definitely not."

Her face softened. "You know I believe in you, Vince, but that's not what matters most. Not quitting is what it really comes down to, and giving everything you've got until the job is done."

He took both her hands and pressed them to his lips. "I love you, Rose Wills."

A sly smile came to her face. "And well you should."

He nodded. And well he should.

NEW ORLEANS HOMICIDE

Monday, February 5

Major Crimes Division
715 South Broad Avenue
Mid-City
8:30 a.m.

Vince arrived at the precinct and made a beeline for the coffeemaker. With a full cup in hand, he went into the conference room. He'd already spoken to Nikki. She'd told him she would be late, which meant he would have some solitude to review the case.

The autopsy was being done before noon, and both Chris Nagle's report and the forensic summary should be in by late in the day. Unfortunately, neither report had been much help in any of the previous deaths except to connect them.

He closed the door behind him and flipped on the lights. The flickering, overhead bulbs revealed a conference table transformed into a sort of filing cabinet laid on its side. Mercifully, Nikki had tasked herself with keeping things organized.

One end of the long table had stacks of papers that consisted of hotline tips. Like the forensic and autopsy reports, they had produced very little useful information.

The other end of the table had the victims' individual folders, each filled with crime scene photos, autopsy reports, forensic results, and neighborhood canvas reports. In between, in the center of the table, Nikki had left a small area clear, big enough for him and Nikki to sit across from each other and work.

He set his cup down and stared at the whiteboard on the far wall. The same list of identifiers was still there, only with a couple updates.

Cause of Death—Exsanguination
Injuries—X-mark at wrist
Age—early to ~~mid-twenties~~ late twenties
No sign of sexual assault, No DNA
~~City~~ Area college students
TOD—three weeks prior to Mardi gras.
Same Positioning—on back with hands crossed over chest, fully clothed
Not eaten in at least forty-eight hours—stomachs empty
Tox screen clear
Ligatures—restraint marks at the knees and elbows, mark on one ankle

No matter how many times he looked at it, nothing popped. He pulled out his chair and sat down. The folder containing the crime scene photos from the country club was waiting for him. He pulled it to him and was about to look it over when the door opened behind him.

"Morning, Vince."

He swiveled to see the lieutenant. "Morning, Ted."

Baker held out a finger with a yellow sticky note hanging off it. "I took this before you got here."

Vince detached the note from his boss's hand. "What's this?"

"McCarty from Tech Forensics called. I didn't have time to take down the details, but she said she had an update for you."

Vince perked up immediately. "Awesome."

Baker stayed by the door, waiting. Vince rotated and picked up the phone. After dialing the number, he placed it on speaker. It rang several times before a now familiar voice came on.

"Forensics."

"Piper?"

"Yes?"

"Vince Wills."

"Oh, hi, Vince."

"You're on speaker. Lieutenant Baker is here and said you had an update."

"I do, I do. The mapping company responded to my request immediately. They got back to me first thing."

Vince's pulse surged at the news. "Fantastic. Anything good?"

"Indeed." Sounds of a keyboard clicking came through the phone from her end. "The rep I talked with said only one search had been done for the Paris Road area inside our timeline. She gave me the ISP number."

The lieutenant moved around to Nikki's usual seat. "ISP?"

Vince smiled. "That was my reaction the first time I heard it. Internet Service Provider."

Baker nodded. "I see."

"So, Piper, can you trace the number?"

"Yes and no. There are several online trackers I can enter the number into, but they only give me the city of origin. I did it anyway and you can guess what I got."

"New Orleans."

"Bingo. The next step is to serve a warrant to the provider, in this case Cox Communications, and request the address."

Baker's eyebrows arched as he started to see the possibilities. "Do you need any help from us?"

"No, I'll serve the warrant from here."

Vince remembered her warning from the other day. "How is Cox at responding?"

Piper sighed. "About like the others—slow."

Baker's face reflected concern. "How slow?"

"Hard to say. Could be a day or two, could be a week or more."

Vince's optimism began to waiver. "Can we push them along at all?"

"Not really. They consider their customers' address and such as proprietary business information."

"Even if there's a serial killer on the loose?"

"I can tell them the situation, but they're a corporate bureaucracy, and behave like one. Nobody wants to make a final decision."

"Okay. It is what it is. Keep me informed?"

"Of course."

"Bye, Piper."

He disconnected the call and looked up at Baker. "That's our best hope right now."

Baker's mood darkened. "Let's hope it doesn't take too long. The window to catch this guy is getting smaller all the time. Fat Tuesday is just a week away."

Vince didn't need to be reminded.

Howard-Tilton Memorial Library
Tulane University Campus
Newcomb Place
11:30 a.m.

He turned off Willow onto Newcomb Place and cruised up toward the library. Finding a spot under a tree, he parked his van and rolled down the windows. From where he sat, he could watch the students come and go from the library's main entrance and determine which ones had driven there alone.

While he didn't have all the time in the world to find the next sacrifice, he'd never missed a deadline yet. There seemed to be no end to the number of women who could serve his purpose. Lunch hour was approaching, so the steady exit from the building would conceal his movement as he chose who to follow.

He checked his watch. 11:48.

The doors swung open, and four students came out together. Two women and two men. He tracked their movements until they reached the parking area. All four got into the same vehicle.

Not them.

Two more students came out, both female, both black. His interest perked up. They walked down to the curb, then turned right and crossed to where the bicycle racks were. Both got on bikes.

Not them, either.

This went on for over an hour. He would see a possible target, only to have her take a bike, get picked up by someone, or walk to the public quad, where he lost sight of her. Starting to grow frustrated, he decided to come back at the end of the day when many more people would be leaving the library.

As he reached for his keys, the doors opened, and two women came out. One was a young lady with her blonde hair in a ponytail, the other black and tall with close-cut curly hair. They walked to the curb and parted ways. His target came toward him then walked by, just feet from his window. Four parking spots back, she unlocked an older, tan Ford pick-up.

He watched her through the rearview mirror, his pulse accelerating as she started the truck and backed up. He started his van and rolled up the windows. Putting it in reverse, he waited for the truck to pass then backed up and followed her.

Her route took them back out onto Willow, then north on Jefferson to Claiborne. The busy road provided plenty of cover, and he trailed her easily. She pulled into a Popeye's drive-thru and ordered some food. He parked at the back of the parking lot until she drove away.

She munched on something from the bag as they drove, and within just a few moments, she turned south on Louisiana Avenue and pulled into the Harmony Oaks apartment complex. He continued past the parking lot, doubled back, and watched as she got out of the truck.

He had found his target.

Major Crimes Division
715 South Broad Avenue
Mid-City
2:45 p.m.

When Nikki had showed up later that morning, Vince had given her the good news about the progress on the ISP. Her reaction mirrored his.

"That's fantastic. How long?"

The question was the most important and least answerable.

He shrugged. "According to Piper—no telling."

Her shoulders slumped. "I hate waiting for something to break, and I hate it most when I can't make my own break."

He laughed. "I hear that."

"What should we do for now?"

"Review notes, I suppose. You go over mine, and I'll look at yours. Maybe we can find something the other missed."

"Better than watching the clock, I guess."

And so that's what they'd done for over four hours, taking only a short recess for lunch.

Regardless of the effort to stay busy, Vince had done a fair amount of clock watching anyway.

The conference room phone rang, and they both stared at it. Vince's pulse surged as he reached for it. Nikki's gaze followed his hand as if he might screw up answering the call. He put it on speaker.

"Detective Wills."

"Vince, it's Chris Nagle."

Nikki slumped back in her chair, seemingly fighting to catch her breath. Vince grinned at her, though he felt the same.

"Hi, Chris. Whatcha got?"

"Diddly squat, I'm afraid. The autopsy on Brandi Cole just wrapped up, and I've got nothing new for you."

Vince sighed, not surprised. "I assume the M.O. matches?"

"It does. Our guy is nothing if not consistent."

"You'll fax the report over?"

"Yes."

"Thanks..." He was about to disconnect the phone when he paused. "Chris, what was TOD?"

"Friday night or early Saturday morning."

His thoughts went back in time to Friday night when he'd been sitting with Rose on the back deck.

"Time's running out," he'd told her.

Sometimes, being right sucked.

"Thanks again, Chris."

He disconnected the call and sat back.

Against his better judgment, he began to picture the case going cold again, him retiring again, and the despair that came with both outcomes. It sickened him.

"Penny for your thoughts?"

He looked up to see Nikki watching him, her head cocked to one side.

"Cost you way more than a penny."

She shrugged. "It's all I got."

He rubbed his face with both hands, trying to erase some of his exhaustion.

"I was just thinking about what happens a week from now if we don't catch this guy."

"I didn't think Rose let you think like that."

He smiled. "She doesn't, but she's not here right now."

"Well, I am." She leaned forward, putting both elbows on the table and fixing him with an intense glare. "Look, I was the one who called Baker and informed him I thought the Mardi Gras guy was back. And I wanted him to call you, even though he read my mind when I tried to suggest it."

"What's your point?"

"My point is—even if you don't realize it—you weren't asked back because you *would* catch this guy. You were asked to come back because you gave everyone else around you the best chance to find him. You hold no special responsibility to solve this case, and you will receive no condemnation if you don't."

He stared at her, slightly taken aback. Nikki was normally reserved and thoughtful, and he didn't remember seeing this fierce side of her before.

"You haven't been talking to Rose, have you?"

The lines in Nikki's face relaxed noticeably. "I'm just saying that we wanted you here for us, not for you. Catching this guy may fill a perceived hole in your résumé, but what we want most is you here fighting beside us—that's all."

He raised an eyebrow. "That was harsh!"

She sat back. "I'm sorry, it didn't come out like I meant it. I'm just trying to say that your presence on this case reassures us that this department is doing its very best to stop this guy."

He hesitated, letting the words sink in. Rose would be proud of her and angry with him. He smiled. "Thank you."

"No problem. I'm sorry if I crossed the line."

157

He shook his head. "No line crossed, but just for the record, the hole is in my gut—not my résumé."

They were interrupted by the phone ringing. Vince pointed at it. "Your turn."

Nikki smiled and hit the speaker button. "Detective Santiago."

"Yes, Detective. This is Laura Chung at Forensics."

"Good afternoon. How can we help you?"

"Actually, I wish I could help you, but I doubt it." The sound of paper shuffling came through the speaker. "The forensic work has been done on the Brandi Cole scene. Unfortunately, we came up empty on anything new. The report will be faxed over when we get off the phone."

Nikki let out a tired breath. "Okay. Thank you for the call."

"Sorry there's not more. Bye."

Nikki disconnected the call. "Strike two."

Vince leaned forward. "Yeah, but I'm going down swinging."

Nikki smiled. "Me too."

Tuesday, February 6

Major Crimes Division
715 South Broad Avenue
Mid-City District
7:15 a.m.

Vince found Nikki waiting for him in the conference room, and her face told him something was wrong. As soon as she saw him, she stood.

"Glad you're here. We have to get to a scene ASAP."

"A scene?"

She was already past him and out the door. "Possible abduction."

He gave chase. "Okay, but why us?"

"The victim is an African-American female in her twenties."

Vince's stomach twisted into a knot. "You said possible?"

"Yeah. The witness who called 9-1-1 said it appeared as if the girl was forced into a vehicle."

He caught up with her at the elevator. "Where?"

The doors slid opened, and they stepped on. She pushed the button.

"Harmony Oaks Apartments off Louisiana Avenue."

He groaned. "You realize I haven't had my coffee yet."

She nodded. "We all have to make sacrifices."

"Apparently, some of us more than others."

She ignored his moaning.

NEW ORLEANS HOMICIDE

Harmony Oaks Apartments
3320 Clara Street
Central City District
8:30 a.m.

Vince pulled the car up to the yellow crime tape stretched across the parking lot entrance and waited. A uniformed officer approached his window. Vince held up his badge, but the officer recognized him.

"Good Morning, Detective."

He smiled. "Gonna be a nice one."

"Yes, sir. Detective Thibodeaux is in charge."

"Okay, thanks."

The officer lifted the tape, and Vince drove under. Jack Thibodeaux was a good detective, and Vince didn't have to worry about stepping on toes. "Just get the job done" was J.T.'s motto.

Vince found a parking spot next to a police car and got out.

Nikki pointed toward a detective who was talking to a man and making notes. "Is that him?"

"Yeah. You've never met him?"

"No, but I've heard the name."

They headed toward the interview. "He's good people. Born and raised in the city."

"Maybe he'll put in for your spot."

"You could do a lot worse for a partner."

Thibodeaux turned and nodded as they approached. His longer-than-department-standard hair was blond, and his

160

athletic build conveyed the image of a man who took care of himself. His brown eyes radiated an intensity that served him well on the job.

"Vince. Long time—no see. I thought you were off fishing."

He smiled. "A common misperception. Jack, this is Nikki Santiago."

Jack nodded. "Nice to meet you."

"Likewise."

Jack, who had apparently been advised they were coming, gestured toward the witness.

"This is Eric Floyd. He called it in."

Vince extended his hand to the gray-haired man, whose wide eyes revealed he'd been shaken by what he'd witnessed.

"I'm Detective Wills."

They shook. "Eric."

"I know you went over it for Detective Thibodeaux, but would you mind telling us again?"

"Sure. I was coming out to my car to leave for work when I heard shouting."

"Where from?"

Floyd pointed at the far end of the parking lot, where more crime tape flapped lazily in the morning breeze.

"Over by the dumpsters."

"And where were you?"

"Right here." Floyd touched the silver Chevy Malibu next to him. "This is my car."

Vince judged the distance to be nearly a hundred yards. "Okay, continue."

"Anyway, the lighting isn't great, but it seemed like she was being pushed into the open sliding door of a van."

Vince and Nikki exchanged looks. This was the first time they'd ever had a vehicle description of any kind. "A van?"

"Yeah, you know, like a panel van."

Vince's adrenaline was pumping now. "What color was it?"

"Not sure, blue or brown, maybe."

"Was there any writing on it?"

Floyd looked toward the spot, as if trying to recreate the images. "Not that I remember seeing."

"What about the people?"

"She was black, but he had a hoodie on. I couldn't see any detail about him."

Nikki had her pad out. "What about the color of the hoodie?"

"Gray, I guess."

"And his pants?"

"Jeans, I think."

Vince turned to Jack. "Have you identified the girl?"

"Yes. Twenty-four year old Jasmine Upshaw. That red Dodge Dart near the dumpsters is hers. It was sitting with its door open and the interior light on. A purse on the passenger seat contained her ID. She was apparently surprised from behind and dragged to the van."

He turned back to Floyd. "Did you hear anything said?"

The man shook his head. "Just the scream. Then I gather he covered her mouth. They were too far away to do anything, but I called 9-1-1 immediately. It all happened so fast."

"I understand. Thank you for your help." He turned back to Jack. "We'd like to have the car processed, just in case he touched something."

He nodded. "Fine with me. Is there anything else I can do?"

"If you'd organize and oversee a canvas of the complex, that would be great."

"Consider it done. Nice meeting you, Nikki."

"Same here. Bye."

Vince headed over to the red car with Nikki in tow, leaving Thibodeaux with Floyd.

"We need to call for a wrecker and have this impounded."

Nikki took out her phone. "I'm on it."

Vince leaned into the car and surveyed the interior. It was clean and fairly orderly. Two textbooks laid on the back seat, partially covered by a Tulane University backpack. He wasn't surprised.

He stood as Nikki hung up. "Wrecker's on the way."

Vince pointed at the back seat. "Look at that."

Nikki peered through the back window. "Tulane student?"

"It appears so."

"That about cinches it."

"I think so."

"Detectives!"

Vince and Nikki turned to see an officer standing in the grass next to the dumpsters. He waved at them. "Got something over here!"

They walked over to where the officer stood and looked down at the ground. A cell phone glinted in the sun.

Vince kneeled, pulled gloves on, and picked it up. The phone came to life when he touched it. A selfie of a young woman filled the screen. Her green eyes sparkled as she smiled widely at the camera. Her black hair was straightened and fixed to shoulder length, where it lightly brushed a blue, off-the-shoulder gown. He showed it to Nikki. "Could be her."

She nodded. "Age and race match."

He touched the screen, and much to his relief, it wasn't locked.

He checked the last number called and found it listed as *Nana and Pops*. The time of the call was nine-thirty the night before. He read the number aloud so Nikki could write it down.

He replaced the phone and looked at the officer. "When forensics gets here, have it photographed then bagged."

"Yes, sir."

He looked at Nikki. "Let's see if Jack has learned what apartment she was in."

****

Over an hour later, they had located the onsite manager, determined which apartment belonged to Jasmine Upshaw, and had gained access to the unit.

Vince and Nikki entered and turned on the lights. As he moved through the living room toward the bedroom, Nikki went into the kitchen. Like the car, the small apartment was clean and tidy. More textbooks were on the couch, and only a TV remote lay on the coffee table.

In the bedroom, he found a framed photo of three people. One of the individuals matched the selfie in the phone, which seemed to confirm the device belonged to Jasmine. The other two were older, possibly her mother and father. He picked it up and removed the picture from the frame. Printed on the back was *Nana and Pops—thirtieth anniversary.*

He kept the picture and went into the bathroom. There, things were in more disarray, probably from the rush of getting ready to leave. The shower curtain was open, an unplugged curling iron sat on the counter, and a towel laid on the floor.

A hairbrush caught his eye. He pulled out an evidence bag and dropped it in. The hair could be used to identify a victim, if that was necessary. He forced himself not to dwell on the possibility.

Nikki was waiting when he came back into the living room. "Just an empty cereal bowl in the sink."

He handed her the photo. "The phone selfie matches. We need to contact her parents."

"Copy that."

Major Crimes Division
715 South Broad Avenue
Mid-City
11:00 a.m.

Back in the conference room, Vince dialed the number for Jasmine Upshaw's parents for the second time. Once again, the call went to voicemail. He left another message.

Nikki had left the room, and when she returned, she was carrying a sheet of paper. She handed it to Vince. "This is the flyer sent to all the media outlets."

It looked like every other missing person flyer they produced, with two exceptions. The first was the bold, red lettering, indicating Jasmine was believed to have been kidnapped, and second, the reward tied to the Mardi Gras Killer would be applied to information regarding the abduction.

He stared at the photo, the same one from the missing girl's phone. Surely, the Mardi Gras connection would start a new round of tips. Vince hoped one of them would be useful.

His ringing phone broke his concentration.

"Detective Wills."

"Detective, this is Gordon Upshaw. You left a message for me to call you."

"Yes, sir. It's about your daughter, Jasmine."

"Granddaughter, actually. Her mother was killed in a car accident when she was eight. My wife and I raised her. Is she okay?"

Vince's throat constricted. It was always more difficult to inform someone of a tragedy when they've already suffered one. Like pouring salt in a wound.

"Sir, do you and your wife live in New Orleans?"

"No. We live in Monroe. Why?"

Monroe was in the northern part of the state, almost five hours away. There was no option. He would have to give them the news over the phone.

"I'm afraid I have some disturbing news about Miss Upshaw."

"Out with it, Detective. I'm not getting any younger here."

He appreciated the man's bluntness. "We believe Jasmine was kidnapped this morning."

"Kidnapped! Why would anyone kidnap my granddaughter?"

Vince considered his next words.

Should he mention the Mardi Gras killer? Apparently, either Upshaw hadn't made the connection, or he hadn't heard about the case. Would tying the disappearance of the man's granddaughter to the case make any difference, or would doing so just increase the anguish he and his wife would go through?

Vince opted for caution. "There have been other cases similar to your granddaughters. We believe it's the work of one man."

Upshaw relayed Vince's words to someone in the background, presumably the man's wife. He came back on, his tone even and direct. "What happened to the other women?"

"They were found deceased."

"You mean they were murdered."

"Yes, sir, but that is not the case with Jasmine, as far as we know right now."

"Do you think you can find her in time?"

That was the million dollar question, wasn't it? And what was the answer? Could he find her before it was too late? If he said yes, would he be lying about his own feelings? And if the answer was no, he couldn't exactly tell Gordon Upshaw that.

Rose and Nikki's words came back to him, and he pushed his negative mindset away.

"We will stop at nothing to find her, sir. There is a city-wide bulletin in place, a reward has been offered, and we have a potential electronic trail. We're doing everything we can."

"We appreciate that, Detective. Is there any way we can help?"

"You talked with your granddaughter last night, is that correct?"

"Yes. She was planning on driving up here for a few days."

"Did she mention anything out of the ordinary?"

"Such as?"

"Someone bothering her, maybe following her."

Vince waited while Gordon and his wife spoke to each other, their voices barely audible. After a few seconds, Gordon came back on the line.

"Neither of us can remember anything. She seemed perfectly normal."

Vince closed his eyes, picturing the small bathroom where Jasmine prepared to leave on her trip just hours before. Unless she'd noticed she'd been followed, she probably had no idea what was coming, so what hint could she have given her grandparents?

"That's all I need for now. Please, call us if you hear from Miss Upshaw."

"Certainly. Detective...Wills, is it?"

"Yes, sir."

"Neither my wife nor I see well at night, and since we can't be ready to leave before dark, we'll head down there tomorrow."

"Very well, sir. Let me know when you're in town."

"We will, and thank you."

The line went dead, and Vince hung up. Nikki was watching him.

"Those were the grandparents?"

He nodded. "Jasmine Upshaw's mom died in a car wreck when she was eight."

Nikki moaned. "That's awful."

"If we don't find Jasmine, it'll be loss on top of loss. I don't want to let that happen."

"Me, neither. Where should we start?"

"Let's see if the apartment building canvas has turned up anything. I'll call Jack Thibodeaux."

Lower Ninth Ward
New Orleans
9:00 p.m.

Jasmine lay on her side in the dark room. Enough light came through a crack in the wood over the window to tell her it was still daytime, but that was about all she knew.

The man who'd forced her into the van had not come back into the bedroom since he'd locked her in there, but the longer he stayed away, the better. Besides, his absence gave her an opportunity to work out a plan of escape…assuming she got the chance to get away.

The small room was void of furniture except for the bed. The sheets smelled of someone else's sweat, and the odor of urine filled the air. It hadn't taken her long to figure out who this guy was—the Mardi Gras Killer. Knowing that didn't make things any better, but the information might serve as an advantage later. Maybe she could talk him down where others had failed.

Then again, maybe she was just kidding herself.

The doorknob rotated slowly, and the door opened with a squeak. Her captor flipped on the overhead light and came into the room with a tray. He no longer wore his hoodie, and after getting accustomed to the sudden brightness, she found herself surprised by his appearance.

She had not gotten a good look at him before—but now that she saw him clearly, he looked…normal. Her mind had created an image of a monster. Long, straggly hair and unshaven. Black eyes and dirty hands. Missing teeth and revolting body odor.

Instead, she found herself looking at a young man with short, curly brown hair, chocolate skin, and big brown eyes. He set the tray on the bottom of the bed, revealing his smooth hands and clean fingernails. When he stood up, he pushed his black, plastic-framed glasses up his delicate nose.

He didn't look like a monster—in fact, he could be any of the male classmates she had at school.

"I imagine you're hungry. I made you a peanut butter and honey sandwich."

She stared at him, unable to reconcile the soft voice with the terror he was inflicting on her. He tossed a water bottle on the bed next to her.

Thirsty, she picked up the bottle and checked the lid. The seal hadn't been broken, so she twisted the cap loose and drank the water quickly. The sandwich was a different matter—it could be spiked with who knew what.

Apparently, he sensed her reluctance. "It's safe."

"I'm not hungry."

He shrugged. "Suit yourself. I'll leave it anyway."

He turned to go.

"Wait!" She pushed aside her fear. She needed a way out, and she'd never find one locked up in the room alone. Maybe she could talk her way off the bed.

"I need to go to the bathroom."

He turned back. "I doubt it, unless that water went straight through you."

"It did."

"Then use the floor."

That explained the smell. "Why?"

"Why the floor?"

"No, why…?"

"Why are you here? Why were you chosen? Why am I doing this? Which one?" Obviously, he'd been asked these questions before.

"All of them."

He sighed, seemingly wearied by having to answer her. "You have been selected by me at random because I had to find someone to be the sacrifice that keeps people safe. There—that's all three answers in one sentence."

"What is the sacrifice for?"

"You don't need to know that."

She pushed, looking for a weakness. "If I'm going to give my life, I have a right to know."

He cocked his head to one side. "You wouldn't understand."

"Okay, but why do I have to spend my last hours tied to this bed? Can't I at least be in the living room?"

For the first time, the evil in him revealed itself. His lips curled into a sneer, and he laughed, a sound born not out of humor, but from a darkness inside him. It chilled her to her core.

"Eat your sandwich."

171

NEW ORLEANS HOMICIDE

The door slammed, and she was alone again. What water she had drank now came out as tears.

<u>Wednesday, February 7</u>

Major Crimes Division
715 South Broad Avenue
Mid-City
7:00 a.m.

Vince, Nikki, and Ted Baker sat around the conference table, each person cradling a cup of coffee as if it contained their life blood. After a long night of following up on fruitless leads from new phone tips, Vince wasn't sure if he was supporting the cup, or the dark liquid inside was holding him upright.

He'd arrived home well after three in the morning, grabbed a few hours of shuteye, then showered and returned to the precinct. Now, they were going over another batch of tips prompted by the morning newspaper. The process was proving just as pointless as the phone tips the day before.

His phone vibrated in his pocket, and he pulled it out and answered the call. "Detective Wills."

"Vince, this is Piper McCarty."

His gaze flipped up to Nikki and Ted. They were both watching him. He mouthed the name *Piper*.

"Hold on, Piper. I'm going to put you on speaker."

"Okay."

He punched the button and laid his phone on the table. "Detective Santiago and Lieutenant Baker are with me."

"Good morning, sir. Hi, Nikki."

They chimed a "Good morning."

Vince got to the point. "You have news, Piper?"

"I do."

"Go ahead, then."

"Well, unfortunately, there's not much to it. I just heard from a Cox Communications rep."

Vince's chest tightened. "Your tone isn't making me feel very hopeful, Piper."

"With good reason, I'm afraid. He told me it'll be a week to ten days before we can expect a response to the subpoena."

Vince closed his eyes tightly and resisted the urge to pound the table. Nikki groaned. Baker seemed to be the only one who didn't grasp the reality of the news.

"Why not? They can't stall like that!"

"I'm afraid they can, sir."

"How?"

"They consider the information we're requesting to be proprietary and therefore, don't release it easily."

"Can't we get a judge to order it done faster?"

Vince hadn't considered the possibility, and the idea seemed reasonable.

Apparently, Piper had anticipated the question. "Yes, sir, we can. The problem is the court process. By the time we file for the order—and assuming Cox doesn't argue it before the judge—it will likely still be three or four days from now."

Baker was adamant. "That's better than ten days."

Piper, to her credit, remained calm. "Indeed, but we run the risk of irritating the company's lawyers. If they decide to appeal, it might be months before we get the information."

Vince opened his eyes to see Baker's unbelieving glare focused on the phone. The wind had quickly gone out of the lieutenant's sails.

"So, what you're saying is that we're better off playing nice, is that it?"

Piper sighed. "That's been my experience, sir."

Baker slumped back in his chair, defeated. Vince reached for his phone.

"Okay, Piper. Thanks. Let us know if you hear anything else."

"Sorry, gang. Bye."

He disconnected the call and stood. Everything that could go against them had done just that. Their situation was worse now than the day he came back. An overwhelming urge to be alone came over him.

"I need some air."

Leaving the conference room, he walked to the stairs, and took them up instead of down. Within moments, he was out on the roof of the precinct. He'd never told anyone this was his favorite place to get away.

Moving over to the south side of the building, he could see the Mercedes-Benz Dome, just a dozen blocks away. Beyond that, the Mississippi River snaked along the southern regions of the city. He leaned against the retaining wall and stared into the distance.

Somewhere within his range of vision, someone was holding Jasmine Upshaw hostage, and the invisible clock was ticking down the hours remaining in her life. His best hope of finding her in time had just exploded in his face, leaving behind a sense of desperation.

Somehow, he had to find the key. He wouldn't accept her death until it was a fact, and experience told him she was still alive. Just over five days remained before Fat Tuesday, the last day they'd ever found a victim.

As the sun climbed higher in the sky, the day warmed, and his resolve hardened.

He had just those five days left to find her, and those same five days left in his career.

When he used to play sports as a boy, his father would give him the same piece of advice before every game. "Leave everything out on the field, son."

That's what he intended to do now—leave it all on the field.

He turned and headed back inside. There was work to do.

Lower Ninth Ward
New Orleans
10:15 a.m.

The door opened so quickly she jumped, pulling on the chain around her ankle. Pain shot up her leg from the open sore she had produced while trying to get free. No matter how she twisted or pried at her leg, the cuff wasn't coming off. She would have to find another way.

He came to the bed, grabbed the plate, and turned to go. She called out, surprised by the weakness in her voice.

"What's your name?"

He stopped but didn't turn to look at her. "It doesn't matter."

"Maybe not to you, but it does to me."

"Why?"

Good question. She couldn't say it was because if she escaped, she wanted to be able to identify him.

"I don't know. I guess maybe I'll feel a little less afraid."

Now, he looked at her, but there was no sympathy in his eyes. "Marcellus."

"That's interesting. What's your last name?"

He shook his head and left the room before she could say another word, but she had something. A name to put to the face…if she could just get loose.

Major Crimes Division
715 South Broad Avenue
Mid-City
2:30 p.m.

Nikki had gone in search of more coffee, and Vince was going through the last of the neighborhood canvas sheets sent over by Jack Thibodeaux when his phone rang.

"Detective Wills."

"Uh, yeah. This is Tony down at Impound."

"Hi, Tony. What can I do for you?"

"Uh, yeah. I just got a call from a guy named Harvey Calhoun, and he was asking about one of our cars."

"Okay. Which car?"

"A blue VW that's listed as tied to one of your cases."

"That's right. The Callie Pearson investigation."

"Uh, yeah. That's it. Anyway, he says the car belongs to him, and he wants to pick it up."

The name Harvey Calhoun didn't ring any bells with Vince, and the only person he could think of who might want the VW would be Andy Pearson.

"Did the caller leave a number, Tony?"

"Uh, yeah. I got it here somewhere."

Vince waited then wrote down the number when Tony rattled it off.

"Don't release the car unless you hear from me directly, okay, Tony?"

"Uh, yeah."

Vince hung up and dialed the number off his notepad. It was picked up on the second ring.

"Cajun Motors. This is Harvey."

"This is Detective Wills with the New Orleans PD. You're Harvey Calhoun?"

"Yes, sir. How can I help you?"

"I received a call from our impound lot that you wanted to pick up a car."

"That's right. The VW belonging to Callie Pearson."

"I'm afraid that vehicle is still being held for evidence. Did Andy Pearson ask you to pick it up?"

A chuckle came through the receiver. Apparently, Harvey found the question funny. "I guess you could say that. He told me he didn't care what I did with the car. He didn't want to see it."

Sensing there was more to the story, Vince decided to visit the car lot. "Where is Cajun Motors located, Mr. Calhoun?"

"1700 North Rampart."

Vince placed it in his mental map. "I know where that is. All right if I come by and chat?"

"I'll be here until six."

"Good." He hung up and went in search of Nikki.

****

Vince had asked Nikki to drive while he tried to get a hold of Andy Pearson. His first effort went to voicemail, but the second time around proved the charm.

"Hello?"

"Mr. Pearson?"

"Yes. Who's this?"

"Vince Wills, New Orleans PD."

"Hi, Detective. You just caught me heading out the door. Do you have news on Callie's case?"

The hope in people's voices when he called, which so quickly disappeared when he had nothing new, always saddened him.

"I'm sorry, sir, but I don't. I do have a question for you, though."

"Of course."

"Did you speak with a Harvey Calhoun from Cajun Motors?"

"Yeah. This morning. Why?"

"He said you didn't want your daughter's VW, and he could have it. Is that correct?"

"Yes."

"Can you tell me the connection between Mr. Calhoun and your daughter?"

"Sure. That's where Callie bought her car. She financed it from Cajun Motors."

Vince chastised himself for not thinking of that sooner. "I see. And did you sign any paperwork for your daughter?"

"No. I offered to help her, but she wanted to build her credit."

"So, why did Calhoun call you?"

"I was listed as my daughter's emergency contact. When she missed her latest payment and he couldn't get a hold of her, he called me."

That made sense, which made it more and more unlikely that Calhoun would be a good suspect.

"You told him you had no interest in the car?"

"That's right. He said when she missed a payment, he'd checked and found the car was in the police impound. He wondered if Callie was in trouble, and if so, was I going to make the payment for her."

"Did you tell him what had happened?"

"No. I didn't feel it was any of his business. I simply told him she wouldn't need the car, I didn't care what happened to it, and he could have it back."

"Okay, Mr. Pearson. Thank you for your time."

"Sure. Are you getting any closer to catching the guy?"

"Nothing solid yet, but we're not giving up."

"I appreciate that."

The line went dead just as Nikki parked outside Cajun Motors. Like many small car lots around the city, the building had begun life as a gas station, but was now devoid of the pumps and surrounded by chain-link fence to keep theft down. Painted above the old service station doors was the name *Cajun Motors*, followed by the words *Buy Here—Pay Here*.

Vince stared at the office, which seemed pointless to visit now. Nikki opened her door then paused.

"Are we going in?"

He shrugged. "There's really no point. Andy Pearson said his daughter bought her car here, that was all. There's nothing suspicious in him wanting to repo it."

She closed her door. "Okay, then…"

From deep inside, something crawled up Vince's spine, into his head, and finally made contact with his brain.

"Wait a second!"

"For what?"

"Andy Pearson said that when Calhoun checked, he noticed that the VW was at the police impound."

"Yeah. So?"

He stared at her. "Checked what?"

She scrunched her forehead. "I don't know, maybe the car had—"

Her eyes widened, and they both leaped from the car at the same time. Their doors slammed in unison, and they went bolting into the car sales office. Vince led the way.

A man in his late fifties with white hair and a polished smile looked up in surprise.

"Can…can I help you?"

Instead of his badge, Vince extended his hand. "Harvey?"

"Yes."

"I'm Detective Wills. We spoke on the phone."

Harvey stood and shook hands. "Yes, of course."

Vince gestured at Nikki. "This is my partner, Detective Santiago."

Another big smile. "Nice to meet you, Detective."

"Likewise."

Harvey pointed at the chairs in front of his desk. "Have a seat."

Vince ignored the offer. "Actually, I have a question for you."

"Okay, shoot."

"How did you know Miss Pearson's VW was at our impound lot?"

Harvey lowered himself the rest of the way into his chair. "GPS, why?"

The three letters hit Vince like a lightning bolt. "Does that GPS track the car continuously?"

"Sure. I don't generally track the cars unless I need to repo one, but the information is part of the program."

Vince took a deep breath, desperate to ask the next question but afraid to hear the answer.

"Can we look at the history on the VW?"

Harvey shrugged. "Sure, I guess."

Vince wanted to kiss the man.

While Harvey tapped on his keyboard, Vince turned to Nikki.

She was right with him in his thinking. "We suspect the car was taken from Couturie Forest with Callie and Brandi inside then returned later that night."

He nodded. "Let's hope we're right."

Harvey tilted his computer monitor toward them. "Here it is. How far back do you want to go?"

"Sunday, January 28."

Harvey hit a few more button on his keyboard, and a map popped up. He pointed at a green line that seemed to wander around the city.

"That's the track of the VW for the whole day."

Vince stared at it, but it didn't make sense to him.

"What are these points that break the line?"

"Pings. They correspond to a particular time in the printout."

"Can you run that for us?"

"Sure."

He pushed yet another key, and the printer on the desk came to life. Five seconds later, Vince and Nikki were staring at a timeline of the car's movements. Vince ran his finger down to six in the evening.

"Can you show us where this ping is?"

Harvey checked it then pointed to the map. "Just east of City Park."

"Then where does the car go?"

With a practiced eye, Harvey traced the path. "South on Saint Bernard, east on 39 all the way to the Lower Ninth. Then she turned north on Tupelo."

Vince's heart was pounding. "Does the car stop?"

"Yeah. Corner of Tupelo and Florida Avenue."

Vince smacked the desk with his palm. "That's him, it's gotta be!"

Harvey stared at Vince as if he'd lost his mind. "Him?"

Nikki was grinning. "Never mind. Can you print the map as well, please?"

"Sure."

Another few key punches produced another sheet of paper from the printer.

Nikki grabbed it and headed out the door. Vince extended his hand again and shook with a startled Calhoun.

"Thank you, sir, very much. When I have time, I'll try to stop by and explain everything to you."

Harvey nodded. "Uh…okay."

Vince beat a path after Nikki, who already had the car started and in drive.

NEW ORLEANS HOMICIDE

Lower Ninth Ward
New Orleans
4:45 p.m.

Nikki turned on Tupelo and cruised toward the target intersection. The last thing Vince wanted was to spook their suspect before he and Nikki were ready to take their guy down. He stayed low in the car as they approached the house.

As they checked the house numbers on the scattered houses, his mind did a balancing act, alternating between hoping they were onto the guy and fearing they were too late. His tension was elevated by the possibility of being detected and forcing the killer's hand, which might end Jasmine's life.

The Lower Ninth ward, one of the hardest-hit areas from the levee failures, was still recovering. Entire blocks, once filled with homes, were now empty lots of overgrown scrub and grass. In many cases, the only evidence a home once stood there was the concrete slab that hadn't been washed away.

As they approached Florida Avenue, only one house occupied the lot between Law Street and Florida. It sat on the corner of Florida and Tupelo—they'd reached their target.

As they approached, Vince realized how perfect a location it was to keep someone hidden. The far side of Florida Avenue consisted of a wide swath of green space that ran parallel to Main Outfall Canal. Behind the house were empty, overgrown lots, and beyond them, a non-functioning power station. You could scream as loudly as you wanted to and probably not be heard.

The home, a small, single-story structure reminiscent of the old shotgun homes, appeared to be cared for, if not lavish. An attached, one-car garage was closed, and the curtains were drawn tight over all the windows. From the front, it seemed no one was home.

Nikki reached the end of Tupelo and turned right on Florida, allowing them to get a look at the back of the house. Again, the lawn was mowed, but other than that, no landscaping or patio furniture was evident. Nikki continued down the street until she passed the power station, then she circled back.

This time, she continued past Tupelo for several blocks before she stopped. "What do you think?"

Vince was convinced. "The layout is perfect. He wouldn't attract any attention down here."

"Agreed, but now what?"

"I wrote down the address. Let's run it."

He picked up the radio. "Dispatch, this is Detective Wills."

"Go ahead, Detective."

"Request information on the following address. 2699 Tupelo Street."

"Copy that. Stand by."

The interior of the car was thick with tension. They were about to get a name, but was it their killer's name?

"Dispatch to Detective Wills."

"Go ahead for Wills."

"Records indicate the property is owned by a Francis Phillips."

Vince wrote it down. "Can you run the name through our database?"

"Stand by."

Francis Phillips. Probably goes by Frank, a generic and harmless sounding name. Vince had expected something a little more intimidating, but then again, the scariest people in this line of work were the ones who appeared normal, even mundane.

"Dispatch to Detective Wills."

"Wills here."

"The name comes back clean except for a speeding ticket almost two decades ago."

Vince looked at Nikki. "Two decades?"

She shrugged.

Vince keyed the mic. "Confirm that as twenty years ago?"

"10-4."

"What is the birthdate on the DL?"

"10-10-49."

Vince rocked back in his seat. That would make their suspect a senior citizen, not the twenty-something the FBI profile had indicated.

"The address on the DL matches?"

"10-4. His license is expired also."

"Copy, Dispatch. Out."

Vince threw the mic down in disgust. "That can't be our guy. No way."

Nikki agreed. "Can't see a man of that age controlling our victims, most of which were in good physical shape, even if he did have a gun. Surely, one of them would have escaped."

"I think so. Maybe that's the owner, and someone else is renting the house."

"Seems logical."

"Okay, let's find a place to set up and watch the place. Maybe we'll see something that clears this up."

Nikki put the car in drive and circled back. They went a block and a half from the house and pulled off onto the swale.

Vince was satisfied. "We can see the house from here. If someone shows up, we'll know. You have binocs?"

"In the glove compartment."

Vince popped it open and retrieved them. With them, he would be able to read a license plate easily. "So, now we wait."

"Should we let the lieutenant know what's going on?"

"Probably. You want to do the honors?"

She smiled. "Sure. After all, you have the binoculars."

"Good point."

NEW ORLEANS HOMICIDE

__Thursday, February 8__

Lower Ninth Ward
New Orleans
12:30 a.m.

Jasmine dozed off and on. Her dreams, when she was able to sleep, were filled with memories of Nana and Pops: The day they'd learned their daughter had been killed in a car wreck. How they had come to Jasmine, sat her on the side of her bed, and promised everything would be okay—she was going to live with them. They had kept their word.

From that day forward, she'd never felt alone. They made sure to attend her school events, gave her parental advice when she needed it and discipline when she deserved it. But now, if she couldn't get away, they would have to endure another cruel blow. She worried they wouldn't survive it.

The doorknob began to rattle, then something banged against the wall. Finally, the door swung open, and Marcellus came in, pulling something behind him. He flipped the light on.

Temporarily blinded, it took her a minute to realize what he was doing.

"What is that?"

"An inversion table."

"A what?"

"I'm not going into it. You'll see."

A cold chill ran through her. The women before her had died by having their blood drained—that much she remembered—but how? Would it hurt?

He locked the table legs in place then tipped the table at an upward angle. She could tell where her feet and head went by the lettering on the canvas covering. Then it hit her. *Inversion table!* She'd had a friend who talked about using one. It hung you upside down by your feet.

"I'm not getting on that."

He didn't turn around, just kept working on the straps. "We'll see."

His tone was flat, emotionless.

She fought the panic building inside her. "You don't need to do this."

He moved to the door and looked back at her. "You still don't get it, do you? I *have* to do this."

The light flicked off, and he was gone again.

She couldn't see the table, but its presence was overbearing and ominous, sucking the air out of the room and her. She sat next to her own personal death device, a sort of guillotine hanging over her.

Tears began to flow again, this time for the worst reason—she was losing hope.

Surveillance location
Lower Ninth Ward
New Orleans
1:30 a.m.

Virtually none of the neighborhood street lights had been replaced since Katrina, so they sat in darkness, the only light coming from the porch of the house they sat next to. A man had come out around eleven-thirty to ask why they were sitting near his house. Vince told him that it was police business, and they wouldn't be bothering the man or his family. Apparently satisfied, he'd gone back in and had not appeared again.

Because neither Vince nor Nikki had come prepared to do surveillance, they had called for the on-duty patrol supervisor to come by and sit with one of them while the other took a break. That had been around ten. Otherwise, they'd passed the time by checking the clock.

Vince rubbed his eyes, weary from staring at nothing. Nikki tapped his arm.

"Vince—look!"

A light above the suspect's garage had come on, and the door was rising. Vince's heartrate surged. He grabbed the binoculars and watched as a van backed onto Tupelo then headed west.

"The plate is too dark. Let's follow him."

Nikki fired the car, and they tracked their target, careful to stay a discreet distance back. Vince watched the plate through the binoculars, desperately hoping to make it out before they were spotted.

"Closer. I still can't get it."

"Do you think Jasmine is in there?"

"A good question. If she is, we'll need to take him down."

"How would we know?"

"Another good question. Unfortunately, I don't have an answer for that one."

Nikki inched closer, but after just ten blocks, the van slowed and its turn signal lit up. At Claiborne Avenue, he pulled into a small, mom & pop convenience store. Magnolia Market, a single-story structure with no gas pumps and bars on the windows, bore a large sign declaring they were open 24/7.

The driver of the van got out and went inside. Nikki pulled in and cruised behind the van. Vince grabbed his door handle.

"Stop right behind it."

"Why?"

"Just do it. And write down the plate."

"Okay."

She stopped abruptly, and Vince leaped from the car, quickly flashing his pocket penlight through the back windows of the van. In less than five seconds, he was back in the car.

"Go."

She pulled away. "Anything?"

"No. I don't think Jasmine is in there. Get the plate number?"

"Yes. Here."

"Circle back. He may just be picking something up and returning home." He keyed the mic. "Dispatch?"

"Go for dispatch."

"This is Detective Wills. Need a 10-27 please."

"Stand by."

Nikki returned to where they could see the vehicle. They hadn't gotten a look at the driver when he exited, but they were watching intently for him to come back out. Vince's optimism rose as he spotted the young man who got in the van.

"He's about the right age."

"Yeah. What's taking dispatch so long?"

Vince shrugged, and his blood pressure went up another twenty points. The van backed up and left the parking lot.

"Dispatch to Wills. Go with plate number."

"Louisiana plate—Victor-Kilo-Charlie-nine-zero-eight."

"Copy. Stand by."

Their suspect turned down Tupelo toward home.

Vince tapped the dash frantically. "Come on, come on."

"Dispatch to Wills."

"Go for Wills."

"Plate comes back to a Marcellus Phillips."

"Can you run the DL info, please?"

"Stand by."

They were just two blocks from the house.

Nikki was watching Vince out of the corner of her eye. "Should we pull him over or not?"

"I'm not sure!"

"Dispatch to Wills."

"Go for Wills."

"DL is for a Marcellus Francis Phillips, age twenty-seven. Address is 2699 Tupelo."

Vince smacked the dash. The son of the homeowner—it had to be. "Copy. Any priors?"

"Negative."

"10-4 dispatch. Wills out."

Nikki was intent on following her target, her eyes wide from surging adrenaline.

"You think it's him?"

The van turned into the driveway, and the garage door started up.

Vince stared at her, his adrenaline pumping wildly. "Only one way to find out."

Their blue and red lights split the night and filled the block with flashing color. The garage door wasn't up far enough for Phillips to pull in, but it suddenly began to start back downward.

The van's back-up lights came on, and it started toward their car. Phillips jumped out and ran to the garage, sliding under the door just as it reached the ground.

The van rolled into their car before Nikki could move and smashed Vince's door closed.

He pushed at Nikki. "Go, go, go!"

She threw her door open and climbed out of the car, Vince right behind her. Weapons drawn, they ran to the house.

Vince pointed toward the back yard. "Cover the rear, I'm going to the front."

He reached the door and tried the knob. Locked.

Stepping back, he raised his foot and kicked the door as hard as he could. It flew inward with a crash. Vince dipped inside the door and yelled.

****

Running, then the bedroom door smashing open, startled Jasmine awake. Marcellus came bolting in, unlocked her ankle chain, and grabbed her by the wrist. Too surprised to resist and without the strength to walk, she found herself being dragged out the door and down the hallway.

"Police. Show yourself, Phillips!"

Police! Was she dreaming?

"Now, Phillips! It's over!"

She wasn't dreaming. A surge of energy allowed her to pull loose from his grip.

"Back here!"

Marcellus turned and attempted to grab her again but then stopped short.

At the end of the hallway, a man stood with his gun aimed at Marcellus. "Don't move, Phillips!"

Marcellus hesitated, then turned to look at the sliding door to the rear patio. It was open.

Jasmine recoiled against the wall, trying to inch toward the police officer. When she looked toward the door, she saw why Marcellus hadn't made a break for it. Standing with her legs apart, arms raised in a classic shooting position, was a female officer.

"Hands behind your head and down on your knees, Phillips!"

Marcellus remained composed but defiant. "You don't want to do this, Detectives."

The female officer nodded. "Oh, yes we do. Hands behind your head and get down on your knees— now!"

When Marcellus obeyed, Jasmine lunged toward the male officer, who wrapped her in his arms.

Tears flowed down her face. "Thank you."

To her surprise, the officer was crying, too.

195

NEW ORLEANS HOMICIDE

Major Crimes Division
715 South Broad Avenue
Mid-City
4:45 a.m.

Vince was more tired than ever before. The adrenaline from earlier had drained from his body, leaving him spent. He considered going home and leaving the interview to Nikki but decided against it. This was his baby to finish.

Crime scene techs were still working the house on Tupelo, and Nikki had stayed to help with the search. Marcellus Phillips had been transferred by squad car and put in a holding cell. Jasmine was at the hospital, where her grandparents were going to meet her.

Vince was now waiting for Phillips to be brought to the interview room.

The door opened, and the sound of leg chains tied to wrist cuffs told him that Phillips had shuffled into the room. The guard set the prisoner down in the chair opposite Vince, then left them alone.

The man's defiance from earlier was still in place. "Can I get these off?"

"No." Vince slid a piece of paper and a pen across the table in front of Phillips. "I know you've been advised of your rights, but I'll do it again."

"Don't bother."

Vince shrugged. "Okay. I need you to sign that sheet saying you know them."

Phillips picked up the pen and scrawled across the bottom, his chains dragging on the table. Vince collected the sheet then pointed at the camera behind him. "This session is being videotaped."

"Whatever."

Vince took out his personal recorder, set it on the table, and pressed record. "Where should we begin?"

"What do you mean?"

"Do you want to go in chronological order or some other way?"

"You mean about the women?"

"Yes, about the women."

"They were just essential parts of my mission. It was nothing personal."

Vince opened the folder he brought with him and spread out photos of each victim, placing them on the table in front of Phillips. Eleven photos in all. "The deaths of these women were personal for their families."

"I understand that."

"Why black, female college students?"

Phillips snickered. "Look at me. They were the easiest to approach without setting off alarm bells."

"So you could take them and kill them."

"Yes, but it was for the greater good."

"Whose 'greater good'?"

"The people of the city of New Orleans."

Vince leaned back in his chair. "You killed these women for the good of the city?"

"That's right."

"That might be the strangest reason to be a serial killer I've ever heard."

Phillips chains jangled as he leaned forward, and his eyes flared. "I'm not a serial killer!"

"You are by every definition I've ever heard."

"No! I'm a missionary."

"Missionary!" Vince nearly choked on the word. "For who? Satan?"

The prisoner's face darkened, and his words came out laced with venom.

"Don't ever say that again. I was doing what my father sent me to do."

Vince was beginning to suspect he was on an episode of the *Twilight Zone*.

"Your father? Who is that? God?"

"No. My dad."

Vince thought his head would explode. "You killed these women because your dad told you to?"

"Yes. He came to me in a dream."

"So your dad is dead?"

"That's right."

"And what did he say in this dream?"

"That I'd been tasked with making the blood sacrifice necessary to pay for the sins of New Orleans."

Vince just stared at Phillips. This neat, well-spoken young man had killed eleven women because he thought his dad had given him some kind of holy mission. In all the time Vince had spent considering the motive for the killings, that one had never crossed his mind.

Stalling while he considered his next line of questioning, he gathered up the photos and put them back in the folder. If Phillips was angling for an insanity defense, this might be the best story Vince had ever heard. Finally, he decided that the motive was the key, and, "Daddy told me to do it," was not it.

Fortunately, Phillips seemed more than eager to explain. He sat back and cocked his head to one side. "Where were you during Katrina, Detective?"

"Working the streets. Why?"

"Do you know where my dad and I were?"

"Of course not."

"We were on the roof of our home, fearing for our lives and praying for deliverance."

Vince nodded. "Many people found themselves in desperate circumstances."

"Do you know what real fear is, Detective?"

Vince was quickly losing interest in this line of questioning.

"What has this got to do with the killings?"

"Because fear drove everything my dad did after that day. He worked tirelessly to rebuild the neighborhood, to tell people to repent and trust God, and if they did, it would never happen again."

"I imagine there were a lot of people who hoped the same thing."

Phillips shook his head. "Not hope. My dad came to me in a dream and said if blood sacrifices were made, the city would be safe. The women gave their life so the city would never suffer a catastrophic loss of life again."

Vince became aware of the look in Phillips's eyes—the look of a true believer. He was actually certain he'd saved lives by taking lives.

"What did you do with the blood?"

"Poured it as an offering on the three main levees of New Orleans."

"Why?"

"Why the levees or why did I pour it?"

Vince was getting angry now. "Both!"

"I chose those levees because they were the ones that broke and flooded the city, killing so many. The blood was poured to atone for the sins of the city, Mardi Gras in particular."

"How does innocent blood on a dirt mound protect the city?"

"Hebrews 9:22. Without the shedding of blood, there can be no remission of sins."

Vince wanted to throw up. He stood. "Guard!"

The door opened, and the same officer came in. Vince pointed at Phillips.

"Get him out of my sight."

The guard moved over and took Phillips by the arm, raising him from his seat.

Phillips wasn't done. "Someone will be called to take my place, Detective."

"I doubt it."

"Why?"

"Because there's a scripture more powerful than any you have quoted."

Phillips was resisting being dragged through the door. "What is that?"

"Thou shalt not kill."

Friday, February 9

Home of Vincent and Rose Wills
Memphis Street
Lakeview Neighborhood
North New Orleans
4:00 p.m.

Vince arrived home just as Rose was getting up and around Friday morning. She'd met him at the door, kissed his cheek, and led him upstairs. Gently, she'd removed his shoes, helped him to lie on the bed, and covered him up. He was asleep before she shut the door.

After sleeping for ten straight hours, he'd gotten up, showered, and gone in search of food. She had made him meatloaf and mashed potatoes. Comfort food, and after combining it with three cups of coffee, he was starting to feel human again.

He'd filled her in on all the developments, and she'd cried with him when he told her about saving Jasmine Upshaw.

She'd touched his hand. "I knew you could do it."

Now, he was dialing Nikki's number.

"Hello?"

"Where are you?"

She laughed. "I couldn't think straight anymore. Baker sent me home."

"You did good work, Nikki."

"We did."

"You know if you ever need an ear, I'm here for you."

"That means a lot. Talk to you later."

"Bye."

He hung up and dialed Ted Baker.

"Baker."

"Hey, Ted. It's me."

"How you feeling, Vince? Did you get some sleep?"

"I did. I'll be back to normal in a week or so."

"Listen…" Baker's voice dropped to a whisper. "We owe you, Vince. That guy never would have stopped."

"Nonsense, Ted. I owe you. The last forty-eight hours were the best of my career."

There was a long silence, and when he came back on, Ted's voice trembled. "My best to Rose and the girls."

"Thanks, I'll tell them.

"Talk to you later then?"

"Yes, but Ted, one thing…"

"What's that?"

"Unless you're calling me to go fishing, lose my number!"

Baker laughed. "Done."

John C Dalglish

FAT TUESDAY

Tuesday, February 13

Mardi Gras parade route
Downtown New Orleans
10:30 a.m.

Vince stood along the curb with Grace in front of him, his arms draped over her shoulders. Domm and Alicia were to his right and Rose to his left. The air was crisp but not cold, and the cloudless sky mirrored his mood. His smile had returned, and laughter came easier.

A long time had gone by, nearly four years, since the last time he'd seen a Fat Tuesday parade. It had been a family tradition until the killings started. Even if he had to work a parade route, Rose and the girls would watch from a spot near where he was stationed.

He stole a glance at Rose, whose arm was hooked through his own. Her smile had never left, but it was more peaceful now, more content. He sensed the burden lifted from him, had been removed from her shoulders as well.

Grace let out a squeal of delight as two jesters, adorned in purple, green and gold outfits, came scampering by. He bent over and kissed the top of his granddaughters head.

Alicia, ever sensitive to the moods of the people around her, smiled.

203

NEW ORLEANS HOMICIDE

"It's a beautiful morning, isn't it, Dad?"
He nodded.
"It is indeed."

Author's Note

The City Murders #7 took us to the deep south and into some of the fascinating Cajun culture. New Orleans is a city that continues to struggle with the after effects of Hurricane Katrina, but has rebounded with gusto. It remains a city with much to offer.

On a different note, I hope this novel captured a sense of the impact that the cases they work have on officers and their families. I once heard that "detectives don't work cases, the cases work the detectives."

With a son who works in law enforcement, I am privy to some of what he sees every day, and they are people to be admired. The advent of body cams, meant to expose police corruption, have had a completely different result. The pictures reveal that 99% of the men and women who protect us are honest and hard working.

Finally, to you who take the time to read our novels, we say again, thank you so much. Your reviews and letters keep us going. It is our hope that each new book is found to be worth the time you invest.

Until the ink dries on our next effort, God Bless.

John & Bev
I John 1:9

Cover by Beverly Dalglish
Edited by Jill Noelle-Noble
Proofreading by Robert Toohey

Made in the USA
Middletown, DE
26 March 2020

87311623R00123